# This Time for Always

by

# Debra St. John

This Time for Always

Cover Art by *Angela Anderson*

The Wild Rose Press
PO Box 708
Adams Basin, NY 14410-0706
Visit us at www.thewildrosepress.com

Publishing History
First Champagne Rose Edition, 2008
Print ISBN 1-60154-295-X


Published in the United States of America

## Logan's strong arm encircled her waist, preventing her from falling...

Sharlie caught her breath as her body pressed against him. She raised her eyes to his.

The anger in his eyes turned to awareness. His breath hitched. The temperature in the tiny room rose.

Logan's gaze roamed every inch of her face, finally coming to rest on her lips.

Her pulse quickened, the beat thundering in her ears. They were so close she could feel the cadence of his heart. She sucked in a gasp of air.

His gaze met hers again. "I've tried to stop thinking about you like this. But I can't."

Sharlie licked dry lips, then cursed inwardly when the action drew his attention there once more. His head lowered.

"Don't," she managed.

"Don't what?" Logan's warm breath caressed her cheek.

"Don't kiss me."

"Why not?"

"Because I don't want you to." Even to her own ears the protest sounded weak.

"Liar," Logan taunted.

"Please," she tried one last time, shaking her head in a vain attempt to deny the feelings coursing through her.

Logan cupped the back of her head, stilling the motion. "I have to." His words melted into a kiss as their lips met.

The gentle insistence of his mouth coaxed a response from her. Her lips parted, allowing the kiss to deepen. Their breath mingled. The moist heat made her knees buckle.

"Don't you remember?" Logan's husky voice whispered, as his lips left hers to trail down the column of her throat. "Remember how good it was."

## Dedication

For John, my husband and real life hero, who taught me what love and romance are really all about. I thank God for you. To Neice, thanks for Logan. And to my Chicago-North RWA friends and fellow writers, thank you for all of your support, encouragement, and expert advice.

## Praise for This Time for Always

First place winner in the 2000 "Ticket to Write" contest

"Tension between the characters is seductive."
"Sharlie's likable and believable. Logan's job with kids really helps boost him as someone to be liked."
~Judges' Comments

"Great story. You have a gift of words and the ability to string them together, plus you have hit on a double whammy formula—the cowboy and the secret baby."
~Jackye Plummer, contest coordinator

"Misunderstanding separates two lovers. Trust brings them back together. A perfect blend of small town Western flavor, sizzling romance, and likeable characters. Debra St. John masters the art of revealing just enough to keep you guessing. As you peel off one layer, another presents itself. You can't help but race on to find the answers. A must read from a talented new author."
~Morgan Mandel,<br>author of Girl of My Dreams and Two Wrongs

## Author's Note

Dear Reader,

I am so pleased to bring you *This Time for Always*. It has been a labor of love for many years, and it's a dream come true to see it published. Sharlie and Logan hold a special place in my heart, and I hope they will capture yours as well.

I am a big fan of country music and have loosely based The Corral on the bar where my husband and I met. I have so many wonderful memories of that place, and even though it's gone now, for me it will live on in the pages of this book.

I hope you enjoy reading Sharlie and Logan's story as much as I've enjoyed writing it.

You can visit me at www.debrastjohnromance.com.

Happy Reading!

All the best,
Debra St. John

Chapter One

She had once carried this man's baby.

Sharlie Montgomery fought the urge to cover her abdomen with her hand as she stared across the table at the man who wanted to buy The Corral. Images of him as a teenager raced through her mind, tangling with the image of the self-assured businessman gazing at her. His eyes mirrored the shock she felt deep in the pit of her stomach.

"Sharlie, are you okay?" Pete Sorrenson, The Corral's aging owner, looked at her with concern.

Mentally shaking her head, Sharlie smiled. "I'm fine," she lied, twisting a strand of hair around her finger. What had started out as a nightmare of a day was getting worse by the minute. Not only had she found out that Pete was ready to sell the bar, but it looked like Logan Reed, someone she thought she would never see again, wanted to buy the place.

Looking far from reassured, Pete continued, "All right, then. Let's get started."

Sharlie studied Logan from under her lashes. The years had turned him into a striking man. Sinfully black hair curled where it brushed the top of his collar. His vivid green eyes were framed by long lashes, and he had the rich, even tan of someone who spent most of his time outdoors.

They had once been inseparable. He had been her whole world, her best friend, her everything, until he'd run away, leaving her when she had needed him most. She remembered the pain and felt the awful emptiness inside her soul. What was he doing here now? Did he know about the baby?

"This is my manager, Sharlie Montgomery."

1

She stared in horror as Logan held out his hand to acknowledge an introduction that was unnecessary.

His eyes mocked her as she extended her hand and placed it in his. It had been almost twelve years since she'd touched him last. Then their touches had been much more intimate than a mere handshake.

"You manage this place?"

Logan's familiar, yet deepened voice sent her spinning back into another web of memories. Fighting through the tangled mess in her mind, she managed, "That's right."

"I don't know what I'd do without Sharlie," Pete broke in, a confused expression on his face, as if sensing the undercurrents flowing between the two. "Best decision I ever made was to put her in charge of this place. I haven't had to worry about a thing in years." He smiled at Sharlie, then turned to Logan.

"Based on the information you sent and our phone conversation, I wanted to meet in person to discuss the sale of The Corral. I'd like to talk to you before we bring the real estate folks and lawyers into the picture."

"Well, sir," Logan said. "I'm looking to acquire a property such as this to add to my business holdings. I have no intention of changing much about the place."

Sharlie wondered how a small town boy from the wrong side of the tracks had come to have business holdings when he'd had nothing except the clothes on his back. Of course leaving that small town with a sizable check in his pocket would be a good start. All of the bitterness, hurt, and anger of twelve years ago rushed at her as she listened to Pete and Logan's discussion.

"Now I'd like to—" Logan stopped as his cell phone rang. He frowned at the tiny illuminated screen. "Excuse me. Is there someplace I can take this call?"

"You can use my office," Pete replied. "It's down the hall. First door on your right past the kitchen."

"Thanks."

Sharlie's gaze followed Logan's easy stride from the room before she turned on Pete.

"Now don't look at me that way, honey. We've talked about this. You knew I was going to sell The Corral at some point."

"I know. I didn't think it would be this soon."

"Almost a year has passed since I started thinking about retiring. I've been in this business for over forty years. It's time for me to move on."

"That's fine, but don't sell this place." Especially not to Logan Reed. "I can run things around here. I'm good at it. You said so. You don't need to bring someone in from the outside." Her voice trembled with emotion.

"Now, take it easy, honey. The only thing that's going to change is the owner. Logan Reed is my top candidate at this point. He wants to keep things the way they are. You'll remain as manager. The staff would stay the same."

Work for Logan? Never. "Pete, think about this. Of course Logan, I mean, Mr. Reed, is going to say all of those things. He'll say anything to get you to sell to him. Then he'll take over and do things his way." She pleaded with her long-time boss and friend to understand. "It won't be the same. I know it." She would have to leave. Start over again. "How can you do this to me? This is my home. The people here are my family. I don't have anyone else."

Pete gazed into her eyes for a moment, then reached across the table to take her hand in his. "Please try to understand. I'm not doing this to hurt you. This will still be your home. You won't be going anywhere."

Oh, yes, she would, if Logan took over. She

wouldn't be able to stay. She couldn't stay. "Why don't you sell the bar to me? I can get some money together and..."

Pete shook his head. "Honey, I would love to sell you this place. But you don't have the kind of money it would take. It's time to do this now. I've got a place all picked out in Florida. A fishing boat, too. I need the money from the sale of The Corral to close the deal."

Sharlie looked into faded blue eyes that begged her to understand. What right did she have to expect Pete to put his life on hold while she came up with money she didn't have, and wouldn't have, for a long time? Twelve years ago, before coming to The Corral, getting any amount of money would have been no problem. Then again, twelve years ago she wouldn't have needed money for anything.

In the back of her mind she wondered what her father would say if she asked him for the money. Before the thought could fully form, she pushed it aside. She'd put that life behind her.

"When are you going to make your final decision?" Her voice was strong now, her resolve firm. She could start over some place new. She'd done it before. She could do it again.

"Soon. I'd like to talk with Logan about his plans some more."

"What do you know about this Logan Reed?" She tried to sound casual.

Pete thought a minute, then answered, "He seems sincere. Works in the real estate investment market. He's in town with the rodeo, so I asked him to come in for a meeting. I get the impression he's thinking about settling down here. Used to live around here from what I gather."

"He's in town with the rodeo?" Sharlie frowned. "Logan isn't the rodeo type."

Pete looked at her sharply. "He doesn't ride the

circuit, not in the way you're thinking. He runs some kind of traveling rodeo camp for kids. Sounds like he's pretty good at it. But, he wants to put down some roots, set up a permanent camp around these parts."

This time she gave in to the urge and placed her palm on her abdomen. Logan would be good with children. He would have been great with their child. Guilt washed over her.

Anger set in as she remembered he'd left before he had the chance. "Yeah, well running a kids' camp is a lot different than running a bar. Besides, how do you know this guy is going to stick around?"

"Do you have something against Logan? I get the feeling you don't care for him much."

Sharlie almost laughed out loud. She had once cared for him above all else. And she'd need a long piece of paper to list his sins. Then again, she had a few of her own to add. Pete didn't need to know all of the sordid details.

Logan chose that moment to return, saving her from replying. "Sorry about the interruption."

"Not a problem," Pete assured him. "I was discussing your offer with Miss Sharlie. I'd like you to talk more about it with her."

"What?" Sharlie's gaze flew from Logan to Pete and back again.

"Why don't you show Logan around?" Pete smiled at her, then turned to Logan. "It's about time for this place to get jumpin'. You can see what it's like around here. Miss Montgomery can answer any questions you might have."

"I don't think that's a good idea, Pete. It's going to be a busy night, with the rodeo people in and all, and I'll have a lot to do."

"I promise I won't get in the way, Miss Montgomery." Logan stressed the formal address, mocking her with his eyes once again.

Spend time alone with Logan? "All right." She hoped her panic didn't show. What if he asked her questions she couldn't answer? Questions that didn't have anything to do with the bar.

"Thanks, honey." Pete rose. "I'll talk to you later. Logan, Sharlie will take good care of you."

"I'm sure she will." Logan's eyes held hers, then he turned and shook Pete's hand. "I'll be in touch."

Logan followed her from the room. Before she could make it to the safety of her office, the touch of his hands on her shoulders stopped her. He turned her to face him. His eyes bored into hers for long seconds until he demanded, "What the hell is going on, Sharlie? What are you doing here?"

Although every nerve ending in her body had come alive at his familiar touch, she managed a calm, "Nice to see you again, too, Logan," above the pounding of her heart. "As for what I'm doing here, I thought that was obvious. I work here."

Logan sighed, then removed one hand from her shoulder to run it through his thick, dark hair.

Her heartbeat quickened as she remembered her hands making the same journey so many times. She used to love running her fingers through Logan's silky hair while he lay his head in her lap after—

What was she thinking? She shook free of his other hand.

Logan raised an eyebrow. "Quite an interesting place for Daddy's little girl to be. I'll bet the old man doesn't cotton to his darling working in a bar."

"What my father thinks is no concern of yours. Although having a rich father turned out to be quite an advantage for you, didn't it? How many business holdings do you have?" Sharlie's voice was bitter.

Logan folded his arms across his chest. Anger flared in his eyes. "Ah, yes. Daddy's money. Not much it can't buy, now is there?"

Their gazes smoldered and clashed. Then into the storm came a voice.

"Miss Montgomery?"

Taking a few seconds to pull her attention from Logan, Sharlie took a deep breath and turned to face the young woman who had spoken. "Yes, Pam?"

The waitress looked from Sharlie to Logan as if she could feel the tension in the air. Sharlie didn't doubt it. The air almost crackled with electricity.

"Um, I'm sorry to interrupt you, but I have a question about this tab." She held out a receipt.

Sharlie glanced at the small slip of paper. "This looks fine. Have the customer sign it at the end of the night."

"Thanks, Miss Montgomery." The rookie waitress grabbed the receipt and scooted away.

Sharlie could feel Logan's gaze boring into the back of her head. She turned to face him. "If you'll excuse me, I have a job to do." She started to brush past him, but stopped when his hand gripped her upper arm. Her flesh warmed at once.

"We're not finished."

"Yes, we are. I have things I need to take care of."

Logan smiled, causing her heart to skip a beat. "You have to take care of me. Pete's instructions if I recall. Show me around and answer my questions."

Sharlie stared at him in amazement. "You can't be serious about buying this bar."

"Oh, but I am."

"I don't want you here."

"Well, now. That decision is out of your hands. If you'll wait here for a few minutes, I'll be right back."

"If you're so anxious to see this place, where are you going?"

Logan's hand swept over his attire, and her gaze followed it down the lines of a well-tailored suit. "I don't think I'll blend in down in the bar wearing this.

I've got a change of clothes in my truck."

"I can't wait around for you. I have a bar to run. I'll be downstairs." This time Logan allowed her to pass him. Sharlie felt him watching her descent into the bar.

She leaned on the corner railing for a moment, taking a deep breath and letting the soothing strains of a Chris LeDoux ballad wash over her. Trying to dispel the disturbing images flowing through her mind, she inhaled. The familiar leather and wood scent of the barroom filled her nostrils. She still felt like screaming.

"Son of a—"

Her gaze narrowed as the sound of flesh meeting flesh cut off the expletive that echoed her own thoughts. She glanced to the corner of the bar where Zach and Jake were already on their way to put an end to the ruckus. She smiled.

Her expression changed when she saw Logan descending the stairs dressed in a well-worn denim shirt, form fitting jeans, and black cowboy boots and hat. He looked gorgeous and sexy as all get out. She grew warm under his intense gaze. Did he have to watch her like that?

"Miz Montgomery?"

Tearing her gaze from Logan, she confronted two sullen looking cowboys, each in the hands of her best bouncers.

"These are the two who started the trouble back there," announced Zach, a question in his brown eyes as he looked at Logan, who had come to stand beside her.

"Look, guys," Sharlie began, taking in the bloody noses and knuckles of the pair. "Rodeo time or not, this isn't a fightin' kind of place. You'll have to take yourselves somewhere else if you're looking for that kind of action." She switched her gaze to the lean, blond-haired bouncer. "Jake, be sure they don't come back tonight. Call them a cab if they don't have a ride. It looks like they both have a few under their belts."

"Yes, ma'am." With a wink Jake touched the brim of his hat and led the trouble-makers away.

Sharlie grinned up at Zach, who remained, then saw that his attention was once again directed at Logan.

"Ah, Zach Rawlings, Logan Reed." She made the introduction, then smiled once again at Zach, turning her back on Logan. "Every year it's the same. The rodeo brings out the macho in every cowboy who walks through these doors."

Zach, an answering grin on his face, hooked his thumbs in his belt loops, then curled his lip. "Darlin', I know what you mean." With an exaggerated swagger of his jean-clad hips, and one last glance over his shoulder at Logan, he sauntered away.

Sharlie's light laughter was cut off by Logan's curt, "Who's that?"

"Zach? One of my bouncers. Takes care of unruly customers for me."

"Seems like you're kind of friendly with the hired help."

Logan's sarcastic tone snaked down her spine, but she refused to rise to the bait. "I won't discuss my relationship with my co-workers with you." She turned on her heel, walked toward the bar, and reached around to grab her hat. Doing her best to ignore Logan, who followed in her wake, she surveyed the crowded room.

The barroom was almost filled to capacity. The large space seemed to be wall-to-wall cowboy hats. People crowded around the main island bar and the two side bars, beer bottles close at hand. They walked around several pool tables lining the perimeter of the room, trying to judge the best angle to sink the game winning shot. They glided across the dance floor in the two-step's quick-quick-slow-slow rhythm. And they filled all the places in between. The country fad may have lost momentum in other places, but here it was still going strong.

She would miss all of it if Logan took over. The bar was like home to her. Adjusting her own hat, Sharlie focused on some of the faces beneath the sea of cowboy hats. The dancers gazed into each other's eyes. Win or lose, the pool players slapped each other on the back, congratulating each other on a good game. The bar flies talked and joked in peaceful camaraderie.

Her casual perusal sharpened as she detected trouble at the main bar. She walked over, and Logan trailed along observing every move. She searched out and caught Zach's gaze, nodding her head to indicate he should join her.

"I'm sorry, sir. But like I said, I can't serve you anymore," the bartender was informing a disgruntled patron as Sharlie and Logan arrived on the scene.

"Everything okay here?"

"Howdy, Miz Montgomery." The bartender smiled. "I was telling this cowboy here that he was done for the night."

The man in question turned angry, bleary eyes on Sharlie. "And I've been tryin' to tell thish here bartender that I ain't even closh to being done for the night."

The glaze over his bloodshot eyes and the slight slur of his words told her the bartender had made the right call. Sensing Logan was about to say something, she held up her hand in warning, then turned to the irritated patron. "Sorry sir, but my bartender's right. You are done for the night. We won't serve you anymore. Zach?"

The bouncer spoke from behind Sharlie, earning himself a glare from Logan. "Yes ma'am?"

"He's all yours."

"Thanks." Zach turned to the inebriated customer. "C'mon, buddy. Let's get you in a cab."

"I don't want a cab. I want another drink. I got a right to drink here. I'm a paying cushtomer. You can't do thish. I'll..." The man's protests faded as Zach guided him toward the stairs.

Shaking her head, Sharlie turned back to the man behind the bar. "You definitely made the right call on that one if I do shay sho myshelf." She mimicked a drunken slur.

He laughed. "No problem, Miz Montgomery." The laughter faded into a wide grin. "I always keep a real close watch during rodeo time."

"Don't we all?" she retorted with her own grin. "Fix me a water on the rocks, bartender."

"Comin' right up." In short order an icy glass of water complete with a lemon wedge slid across the bar into her waiting hand.

"Thanks. This hits the spot. Put it on my tab."

"Yes, ma'am."

Sharlie sat down on the stool vacated by the patron Zach had ousted from the bar and finally turned her attention to Logan. She had known he was hanging on every word of the exchange between her and the drunken man and again with the bartender. The disapproval in his gaze made her grit her teeth.

Logan raised an eyebrow at her questioning look. "Yes, Miz Montgomery, ma'am?" His voice mocked the courteous address used around her in the barroom.

She bristled, but said nothing.

"What's with all the drooling cowboys around here?" Logan's gaze raked her from head to toe, his look almost insulting. "Or are they paying homage to the princess, like Daddy used to do?"

His words pierced Sharlie's heart. He had

always spoken so tenderly to her in the past. She didn't care for this side of him at all. She turned away from him, but he walked around into her line of vision again. She fumed in silence, then drew in a deep breath and slowly released it.

She didn't have to explain anything to him. She'd earned the respect Zach and Jake and all of the other employees afforded her. Although if she were honest with herself, she would admit that the "ma'am's" and "Miz Montgomery's" had thrown her for a while, and no number of "Please call me Sharlie's" had changed their minds.

Finally, Zach had explained it to her. "Usin' the proper form of address is the way a cowboy shows respect. And we respect you and what you're doin' here."

That had settled it.

"Refill, Miz Montgomery?" The bartender's voice broke into her thoughts.

Sharlie grinned.

****

Logan couldn't believe it. He had known he would run into Sharlie if he returned, in fact he'd planned on it. One of the reasons he'd returned to the town he'd grown up in was to confront her. Although he sure as hell hadn't expected to find her working in the bar he wanted to buy. And damned if she didn't look like she belonged there.

The crowded barroom and loud country music echoing in his head were a far cry from the society party he'd envisioned meeting her at. His thoughts had centered on her in formal evening wear, not a cowboy hat, fancy Western shirt, and form-fitting jeans that showed off every generous curve. As a teenager Sharlie had been beautiful. Now she was nothing short of drop-dead gorgeous.

He felt a kick in his gut as she smiled at the bartender. She had once looked at him that way.

And he remembered all of that honey blond hair tangled around their glistening bodies, as they lay in the rumpled sheets of his bed. He almost groaned aloud at the memory.

"Miss Montgomery?"

Logan turned as a waitress approached, desiring Sharlie's attention. Pete hadn't been kidding. She did run things around the bar. Everyone looked to her for answers.

The bar seemed like a strange place for her to be. What did her father think about his daughter working with the common folk?

One thing was certain, she had been as surprised to see him as he had been her. For a minute he had seen fear in her eyes. What could she have to fear from him?

Sharlie got up from her stool to walk around the bar, her eyes alert. Logan followed, not saying anything. He knew she was irritated that she had been given the job of showing him around. She didn't want to have anything to do with him. Then again, she had made that clear twelve years ago, he reminded himself bitterly.

That bitterness hadn't abated several hours later as Logan observed Sharlie closing the bar for the night. She had handled everything that came her way with smooth efficiency. With the help of her oh-so-friendly bouncers. They were too familiar with her. He would put an end to that once he took over.

Finally, Sharlie switched off her computer and turned to face him. He'd been waiting while she totaled up the night's receipts. Having him near must be making her edgy. She still twirled the ends of her long hair when she was nervous.

"Well?"

"Well what?"

"How'd we do tonight?"

"We?" Sharlie raised an eyebrow.

"I am going to buy this place." Logan watched for her reaction. He saw the fear along with the shadow of something else enter her eyes again, before she lowered her long lashes to hide the emotion.

"Why, Logan? Why this place?"

"Because it's perfect. It's exactly what I had in mind."

"Yes, it is perfect," Sharlie said, more to herself than him. "Or at least it was."

"Before I came back you mean?"

Sharlie met his stare head on. "That's exactly what I mean." She rose from her chair. "It's late. I need to get home."

Logan came to his feet as well. "I'll walk you to your car."

"That's not necessary. Zach'll walk me out."

Unexpected anger and a deeper, darker emotion flared in Logan's stomach. "How convenient," he drawled.

A matching fire lit Sharlie's eyes, turning them a brilliant blue. "As a matter of fact, it is. If you'll kindly get out of my office?"

He stepped aside with exaggerated gallantry and followed her from the office. His eyes narrowed when he spotted Zach waiting in the hallway.

"Are you ready to go?" the bouncer asked her, casting a speculative look at Logan.

"You bet," Sharlie answered brightly.

Too brightly, Logan thought.

He kept close on their heels as she locked the front door, then turned toward the corner of the parking lot. His eyes narrowed when Zach placed a hand on the small of Sharlie's back. The bouncer's low, "Good night, Sharlie," as he held the door of her small, compact car made Logan clench his teeth.

Her gentle smile and soft reply echoed in Logan's empty heart as he turned on his heel and strode to his truck. Maybe coming back home hadn't been such a good idea.

Chapter Two

Sharlie stepped down from the front seat of the pickup truck and wrinkled her nose at the sharp scent of horse manure. Looking around at the bustle of the rodeo crowd, she smiled, glad she had decided to come.

It had been almost a week since Logan had walked back into her life, and although they hadn't spoken outside of forced pleasantries since he'd stalked away in the parking lot, having him around grated on her nerves. No decision had been reached about the sale of The Corral, but the threat of it hung in the air, suffocating her. Wondering if Logan was going to buy the bar left her feeling raw and open. She hated not being in control, but until the outcome was final, she was stuck.

Wondering if Logan would find out about the baby kept her staring at the ceiling at night. Telltale signs of her lack of sleep showed in the smudges beneath her eyes.

"You set?"

Turning toward Zach, who had finished locking up the truck, she smiled. "You bet."

Coming to the rodeo with Zach had been an annual tradition since the two of them had begun working together. Zach had never made a secret of the fact that he wished they were more than friends. But for Sharlie, that's all they could ever be. Friendship was all she could offer any man. Zach was a good friend. The best. He accepted how she felt, which made him even dearer to her. It also made her wish things could be different.

Since Logan had left, she'd avoided romantic entanglements. She wasn't willing to take the chance of falling in love again. Not that she didn't wish for someone to love and someone to love her in return. She did. More than anything else in the world.

It couldn't happen. Not for her. She might fall in love, but what man would want a woman like her? A woman who wasn't whole.

Looking around at all of the families hurrying toward the grandstand brought a familiar ache. Fingers of pain squeezed her heart at the sight of parents with several children in tow or women with swollen bellies.

She'd had dreams of a big family, too. Those dreams could never come true now. She'd had the chance once, with Logan's baby. Her fear and self-doubt then had robbed them both of the opportunity to know their child. To be a family.

"We'd better hustle if we want to get a good seat."

Zach's words broke into her maudlin thoughts. She gratefully shook them off and nodded.

Finding a spot on the crowded bleachers wasn't easy, but once they were seated, Zach turned to her with a slight frown, tilting her chin up to peer at her face. "You aren't getting enough sleep."

She lowered her eyes. Until the question of the bar was settled, Pete had asked her not to mention anything about the impending sale to anyone. So she kept it to herself and stayed awake worrying about it.

"Nobody sleeps during rodeo week," she said, raising her voice to be heard above the loud country music filling the air. "Too much excitement."

Zach looked as though he wanted to add more, but the loudspeaker crackled to life, and the crowd became silent.

"Ladies and gentlemen! I would like to welcome you to the final days of our rodeo. I ask that you turn your attention to the center of the ring and our beautiful rodeo queen. Please rise and join in the singing of our National Anthem."

Along with the hundreds of others in attendance, Sharlie stood and looked at the beauty queen, decked out in a flashy sequined cowgirl outfit, sitting astride a horse and holding an American flag. All around, cowboys and spectators doffed their hats, holding them over their hearts, as voices rose and blended in harmony, giving honor to their country.

As the last strains faded away, the crowd burst into loud cheers and applause as the Rodeo Queen made one last circuit around the ring on her horse, then cantered off behind the bull riding chutes.

"Hey, there's Jake," Sharlie said, waving at the man donning gear behind the fences.

"I don't think he can see you in this crowd," Zach teased. "From where he is, one cowboy hat looks pretty much like another."

She smiled sheepishly. "I know. I thought—" Her voice came to an abrupt halt as her eyes focused on the activity behind the ring. Logan stood with a group of various aged children gathered around him, and she could have sworn that he was looking at her. But that was ridiculous. As Zach had said, picking anyone out of this crowd would be impossible from that far away.

"Sharlie?"

With effort, she dragged her attention from Logan back to the man sitting beside her.

"They're about to start. You want anything?"

"No, I'm good."

They watched the bareback riders as one by one their mounts were released from the chutes and the cowboys attempted to stay put for the required eight seconds. Steer wrestling followed, and then came time for the kids to take part.

Logan led a rapt group of children, ranging in age from toddler to grade school, into the ring. After a final set of instructions and some encouraging pats and hugs, he turned them loose in the ring where they chased a small calf, trying to grab the ribbon attached to its tail.

The crowd cheered, oohing and aahing as the tiny contestants got close to the calf only to have it slip away to the other side of the ring. Entranced, Sharlie watched along with the rest of the crowd, until her gaze alighted on Logan.

He stood, one booted foot resting on the bottom rail of the fence surrounding the ring, calling encouragement to the kids. Finally, a little girl no more than three or four years old ran toward him, smiling in triumph and waving the blue ribbon for everyone to see. The crowd erupted in a mighty cheer. He swept the girl up in a giant bear hug, then headed into the center of the ring to claim her prize.

"And the winner of our Little Buckaroo contest is Miss Ginny Hawthorne, who wins a savings bond courtesy of Peterson Feed Store." The crowd cheered again as the announcement reverberated through the stands.

A lump formed in Sharlie's throat as she watched Logan with the small girl. He was so gentle with her. He would have made a good father.

She couldn't say the same about herself as a mother. During those long ago days when she'd first found out she was pregnant she'd done a lot of thinking. At seventeen she'd hadn't been ready to raise a child. Hell, she'd been a kid herself.

Logan hadn't been around, and the decision about what to do had fallen solely on her. What she'd done still haunted her, but what kept her awake at night were the events that followed. Would she have done things differently if she'd known how things would turn out in the end?

Her thoughts wandered during the next events, but she responded automatically when the crowd around her cheered a good ride or clapped in encouragement for a bronc rider who hadn't stayed in the saddle. After the intermission, the cowgirls rode in the barrel-racing competition. The most anticipated part of the rodeo, bull riding, was the finale for the day.

"There's Jake," Zach said, pointing behind the fence to where a group of cowboys had gathered. Some of the cowboys stood, others walked around the small enclosure, while still others were relaxed enough to chat. A few bowed their heads in prayer.

The announcer spoke to the crowd as the bull riders prepared themselves to ride. "Rodeo is America's favorite sport. We say this 'cause it comes from the heart of America, right here on her soil. Rodeo isn't derived from any other sport or from any other country. These boys are America, and the sport is from her land."

The first rider was in the chute, almost ready to go. "The bull rider is in no way, shape, or form tied to the bull. The rope lets him get a grip. The rope is held in one hand, and the other hand must be held up over the head. It may not touch the bull at any time." The announcer paused, then continued, excitement lacing his voice. "And our first cowboy is out."

Tension tightened Sharlie's stomach as the bull rider attempted to stay seated on the massive bucking Brahman bull. A collective gasp went through the crowd as the rider was tossed into the air, landing on his back about a yard from the stomping animal. In an instant outlandishly dressed rodeo clowns rushed at the huge creature, drawing its attention away from the fallen rider, who scrambled up and over the fence away from the beast.

The loud speaker crackled again. "Let's give it up for him, 'cause all that cowboy's goin' home with is your appreciation."

Sharlie clapped and hollered, then gripped Zach's hand. "Jake's next."

"Turn your attention to buckin' chute number four," the announcer directed the crowd. "Our bull rider is Jake Hawkins, and he's ridin' Black River. He gives his signal, and he's out!"

Sharlie held her breath as Jake twisted and turned his body to match the wild, spinning creature beneath him. The bull kicked its back legs out, trying to throw the determined cowboy. Jake held on, one hand gripping his rope tightly. The other stayed in the required position above his head. Finally, after what seemed like an eternity, but was only eight seconds, the buzzer sounded. The clowns ran in, allowing Jake to slip off the bull and head for the safety of the fence.

Above the roar of the crowd, the announcer was almost impossible to hear. "Our judges say that's a ride. We'll have his score in a minute."

Sharlie eased her grip on Zach's hand and grinned up at him when they announced Jake's score. "That should get him into the final round tomorrow.

"It should, but there are still quite a few riders left to go."

She waved her hand in a dismissive gesture. "Not a problem."

****

At the end of the day, Sharlie and Zach caught up with Jake behind the chutes while he packed his gear. "I knew you'd do it, Jake. You were incredible." She hugged him, whispering, "I'm so glad you're safe."

"Thanks, honey." Jake winked at her. "And don't

you worry. I know I have to show up for work tonight."

"That's not what I was worried about, and you know it," she admonished him.

"I know, I know. I'm just giving you a hard time. But, hey, I've got to run. I need to stow this stuff and catch up with Janet."

"Well, we wouldn't want to keep you from that, now would we?" Zach laughed. "See you later, man."

"Catch you guys at work."

Jake walked off, lugging his heavy bags. Excitement from the day's events still coursed through Sharlie, and she turned to Zach, hugging him in her exuberance. His arms tightened, holding her close.

She pulled away and out of him arms. "Zach, I—"

"Sharlie—"

Their words tumbled over each other as they both spoke at once.

Her heart tightened at the expression in Zach's eyes. "Please, let me finish," she whispered when he would have spoken. "I'm sorry. I know how you feel about me. I wish I could—"

Zach stopped her words. "I know you do. I understand."

"You shouldn't." Sharlie was angry with herself for not being able to feel anything for Zach and at him for having feelings for her.

"Yes, I should," he said. "You're my friend. And I treasure our friendship. I'd never do anything to ruin it."

"You're a good man, Zach. And I do wish..." They'd had this conversation before, and it always ended the same way.

Zach wasn't the only one. She never let any man get close. She wouldn't take the chance of them wanting something she couldn't give them.

"I know," Zach repeated. He straightened his shoulders. "*I* wish I had something to drink. You thirsty?"

"Parched."

"I'll go grab us something." Zach touched her cheek affectionately, before strolling away to fetch the offered beverage.

Sharlie turned and was startled to find Logan watching her with a hard look on his face. "Logan? I didn't see you standing there." Had he overheard her conversation with Zach?

"Obviously." His voice close to a snarl, he stalked forward.

Backing away from the look in Logan's eyes, she was soon trapped between the fence and his relentless approach. He didn't stop until their bodies were a hair's breath away from each other. She looked around, but saw no one to rescue her. In a crowd of hundreds, everyone seemed to have disappeared, leaving her alone with Logan. Sharlie held her breath, not daring to let the rise of her chest brush against his body.

"Wha— what are you doing here?" She hated the trembling of her voice, but his stance intimidated her.

"Working," was the curt reply. "What are *you* doing here?"

"Zach and I come to the rodeo every year."

"Ah," Logan drawled. "How cozy for you."

He drew a crooked finger down the side of her face, as Zach had done moments earlier. She flinched, burned by the light touch of his flesh on hers.

Logan frowned. "Afraid of me, Sharlie?"

"N...no." She cursed inwardly at her stutter. "Why would I be afraid of you?"

"I'm not sure. Every time I look at you, I see fear in your eyes. What are you afraid of? Are you afraid of me touching you like this? You never used to be afraid. In fact," Logan cupped her face in his hands. "I used to touch you in a lot more places than this." His glittering gaze slid down her body.

She could have sworn he touched her. Her body tingled from his look.

Logan's intense gaze returned to her face, and his eyes hardened. "Does Zach touch you in more places than this?"

"That's none of your business."

"Does he touch you? Kiss you? Hold you against him?" Taking a slight step forward, he brought their bodies together, hard strength meeting curving softness. With one hand still cupping her face, Logan used the other to sweep the hat from her head. "Does he make you feel like this?"

A whimper escaped Sharlie before his lips claimed her mouth. Hot, harsh and demanding, they crushed hers with their moist heat. This wasn't the Logan she remembered. His kisses had been soft and gentle, even in moments of deepest passion. This Logan was almost rough, bruising her lips with the force of his. The kiss was calculating and punishing, but even as she sought to free herself from his degradation, it changed, becoming sensual in its onslaught.

Sharlie was lost. Logan softened his lips, his gentleness coaxing her to respond, and her traitorous body did. She pressed closer to him and clasped her hands around the back of his neck. Her fingers sifted through the dark hair curling over his collar. His spicy male scent intoxicated her, making her head spin. It had been so long since he'd held her like this, but the years melted away as familiar shocks sped along the nerve endings of her body, while her heart beat his name over and over again.

Her lips parted under the insistence of his. Sparks illuminated the dark behind her closed lids.

She felt an echoing flicker deep in her stomach when the tip of Logan's tongue touched hers.

Logan wrenched his mouth from hers and stared into her eyes.

Stunned, she looked into the fiery heat of his gaze. His chest rose and fell in cadence with his harsh breathing. For a brief moment, desire filled his eyes, but then his gaze hardened, and a look that was almost smug replaced the passion.

"Think about that the next time your cowboy kisses you." With a mocking touch to the brim of his hat, Logan sauntered away.

His cruel words pierced her heart, as a sword would wound an enemy in battle. At that moment Sharlie realized that's what they were.

"Sharlie?"

She looked up. Zach stood there, a peculiar look on his face.

"Are you all right? I called your name three times."

She nodded, although her heart beat a fast tempo in her chest, and she stood with her fingers pressed against her lips. Her other hand crushed the brim of the hat she now held. She took a deep breath and uncurled her clenched fist. She hoped Zach wouldn't be able to determine the cause of her slightly swollen lips. Logan had left his mark.

"I'm fine," Sharlie said in a voice that only trembled a little.

"Here's your drink." Zach handed her the icy soda, which she drank in greedy gulps.

"Thanks. This heat is getting to me. Let's find a shady spot and sit for a while."

As they walked toward a grove of trees, Sharlie's mind focused not on the cool relief they would find, but on the liquid heat that still flowed through her veins from Logan's kiss. Passion turned into heated anger, and that fueled her determination. If Logan wanted to be enemies, then so be it.

****

Logan took several deep, cleansing breaths to calm his racing heart. He kicked a fence rail, welcoming the pain that shot up his leg. He cursed himself for being every kind of fool. It took all he had in him not to turn around and beg Sharlie to forgive him.

He cursed again. She wouldn't welcome an apology from him. He'd had no right to kiss her like that, but he'd wanted to make her respond to him like she used to.

She had.

That's when he'd lashed out. His chest tightened at the memory of the look on her face after his cruel words. He'd wanted to hurt her. Hurt her like he was hurting at the thought of her with Zach.

He shouldn't be surprised. She'd made her feelings about being with him perfectly clear all those years ago. Anger coursed through him as he remembered the day in her father's study when he'd been handed a check. A payoff to get out of Sharlie's life.

*"Sharlina feels it would be best if you didn't come around here any more. She asked me to give you this."*

The memory of her father's voice taunted Logan. To this day the pain of her rejection tore his insides to shreds. He'd always meant to go back and confront her about it. To ask why their plans had changed. But it hadn't happened that way. He'd never gone back, and now it was too late to ask. She'd moved on with her life. She was with Zach. Hell, she'd probably had a dozen boyfriends since he'd been gone. Twelve years was a long time.

Before coming back he'd thought about what he would do if she was married. They'd had plans to get married once. The thought of her as someone else's wife made his gut clench.

"Damnit!"

"Logan?"

He whirled at the sound of his name. A sheepish grin twisted his mouth when he spotted Pete. "Sorry, I was thinking out loud."

"Must not be happy thoughts."

"Bad memories."

"We've all got a few of those. Thing is to remember to leave the past where it belongs."

Logan's gaze drifted to the cluster of trees where Sharlie sat with Zach. He closed his eyes.

Opening them, he addressed the gray-haired man at his side. "Do you come to the rodeo every year?"

Pete looked at him out of the corner of his eye and chuckled. "'Course I do. It's kind of required if you live in this town. Your rodeo school should do well here if you decide to settle in."

"I'm thinking of buying the old Dawson ranch."

Pete whistled. "That's a nice chunk of land. And a nice chunk of change."

Logan grinned. "Don't worry. I'm still interested in The Corral." How ironic, to be able to come back to a town he had left dirt poor and be thinking about buying two substantial real estate holdings. Funny how time had a way of changing things.

"How long has Sharlie worked for you?" His gaze sought her out again.

If Pete noted the abrupt change in topic, he didn't comment. "Oh, about eleven, twelve years now." He gave Logan a long look. "Why do you ask?"

"Just curious." Logan shrugged, keeping his tone casual. "She does a good job running the bar. I wondered how much experience she has."

"She didn't have any before she came to The Corral. Poor kid." Pete shook his head. "She came to me with nothin', begging for a waitress job. I took an instant liking to that little lady. Gave her a job and haven't regretted it for a minute."

Logan frowned. "She came to you with nothing? What about her family?"

Pete hesitated, then said, "Sharlie ain't got no kin. We're her family at The Corral. That's why she's so upset about me sellin' the bar."

By the way Pete avoided looking at Logan he knew the older man was lying. He'd bet Pete knew all about Sharlie's past. Knowing that The Corral's owner was protecting her, Logan didn't comment on the evasiveness. He did wonder, though, what had become of Robert Montgomery.

"The bar means the whole world to that gal." Pete's voice broke into Logan's musings. "If you buy the place, I sure hope you do right by her."

"In what way?"

"Keep her on. She's done a heck of a lot for that place. Took on a job not many people would have wanted. Helped straighten things up. Attracted the right kind of crowd. That sort of stuff. I don't know what I would have done without her. She's been my right hand man." Pete laughed, then paused, looking at Logan as if contemplating his next words. "She'll do the same for you. If you treat her right."

****

Pete's words tumbled through Logan's mind as sleep eluded him later that night. Since he'd arrived back in town he hadn't treated Sharlie well at all. It was pure hell, seeing her day after day, knowing she didn't want him around. He hadn't expected his feelings to be so strong. As soon as he'd seen her, it was as though the past twelve years had faded away. The anger he'd held onto all those years paled in comparison to the way she made him feel.

Although if he were honest with himself, he'd have to admit that perhaps his feelings for Sharlie had never gone away. In the twelve years they'd been apart, he'd dated more than his share of women, but when it came to settling down, something always held him back.

As much as he wanted a big family, being married to someone besides Sharlie didn't seem right. It bothered him that he hadn't been able to move on with his life.

Something else bothered him. He couldn't figure out why she seemed to be afraid of him. He'd never hurt her.

Except today. His words and actions had caused her pain. He'd seen it in her eyes.

He'd seen something else there, too. She'd been aroused by his kiss, and for a moment she'd responded to him as she used to. It had felt so right to hold her in his arms.

The memory of her warm lips beneath his caused him to shift under the suddenly too-warm sheet. He punched the twisted pillow beneath his head and cursed. He had a long night ahead.

Chapter Three

"Did you have a good time at the rodeo?" Pete greeted Sharlie as she walked into The Corral the next day. The night before had been busy, and she hadn't had the chance to talk with him much.

"The rodeo's always fun," Sharlie hedged. She had been having a good time until Logan had showed up and devastated her with his kiss. The day had lost some of its shine after his cruel words.

"How about you?" She headed toward her office. Pete followed.

"I love the rodeo."

She nodded and sat behind her desk. Not wanting to dwell on yesterday's events any longer she said, "Well, I've got to get started with this." She indicated a stack of papers. "I'm going to work on inventory for a while."

"Super. I want everything up to date for Logan when he takes over."

Sharlie grimaced.

"Something wrong?"

"What? Oh, no, I'm thinking about what has to be done."

Pete didn't look convinced. "You've kept everything up to date. It shouldn't be that big of a job."

She didn't know what to say.

"Logan was asking about you yesterday."

"What?" Her head snapped up.

Pete propped one hip on the corner of her desk and sat down. "He wanted to know how long you've been working here."

"Oh."

"And he asked me about your family."

Sharlie fought against the rising panic. "What did you tell him?"

"That you didn't have any."

She exhaled the breath she'd been holding, and hoped her relief didn't show on her face. That's what she'd told Pete when she'd come to work for him, but she often suspected he knew the truth.

"He seemed mighty interested in you. Any idea why that is?"

She lowered her eyes and shook her head. "No."

Pete sat in silence for a while, and when she sneaked a glance at him, he seemed lost in thought. "You know I think of you as a daughter," he finally said.

"Yes," Sharlie said, her eyes misting.

"If you ever need anything, or if there's something you need to talk about, you know you can come to me, right?"

"I do know that." Pete treated her better than her own father ever had.

He rose. "Yeah, well, remember I'm here for you. Zach and Jake, too. We're your family, and we'll be here if you need us."

Not wanting to embarrass them both, she cleared her throat and willed herself not to cry. "Thank you."

****

Right before opening that night, Sharlie sat at the bar. Logan walked down the stairs. Their gazes met across the room. As he approached, his searched hers. Drawing near, his glance slipped to her mouth, then back up to meet her eyes. The memory of his kiss assaulted her, and she looked away. But not before she'd seen the knowing look in Logan's eyes.

"We all set for tonight?"

She hated that Logan was part of the operation

31

now. Each day he became more and more involved in the day-to-day running of the bar.

"About yesterday," Logan began.

Before he could finish his sentence, Jake strolled over. Sharlie silently blessed the man. She didn't want to talk about what had happened yesterday.

"Bet we'll have a crowd tonight," the bouncer commented.

"Yeah, one more day for the rodeo," she answered.

"Your kids did well yesterday," Jake said to Logan.

"They sure did," Logan said, pride evident in his voice. "You did well yourself. First place. Congratulations."

"Thanks."

"How long have you been competing?"

"Just a few years."

"Do you ride the circuit?"

Jake shook his head. "Only local events for now. I'd love to ride the circuit someday. How about you?"

Sharlie was curious to hear Logan's answer. He hadn't paid much attention to the rodeo when he'd lived in town.

"The rodeo caught my eye one day. I've been traveling with my camp for a few years now."

"It's a great idea. Good luck with it."

"Thanks, I love doing it."

Jake left, leaving Sharlie alone with Logan. Something she didn't want. But she was still curious. Logan's answers to Jake hadn't satisfied her.

"What's with the rodeo thing now?" she asked. "You never showed much interest in it. This whole town goes crazy during Rodeo Week, and you couldn't have cared less."

Logan shrugged, and the action drew his shirt tight across his broad shoulders. "I guess I was more interested in the blond-haired, blue-eyed girl in my chemistry class."

"Don't," Sharlie warned, noting the look in his eyes. Why had she started this conversation?

"Why not?" Logan asked. "Why don't you like to talk about the past?"

"Because it's over and done with. We've moved on." And it hurt too much to think about.

"What about the future?"

"What?"

"Is it all right to talk about the future?"

"We have no future." She had seen to that. She had no future with anyone.

"Ah, but that's where you're wrong. We're going to be working closely together here at The Corral."

"Not if I can help it," she muttered under her breath.

Logan folded his arms across his chest. "Okay, we won't talk about the past or the future. Let's talk about right now."

Behind Logan, Sharlie caught a glimpse of the first customers descending into the bar for the night. Saved again. She turned away from him. "Right now I have a bar to run."

As she walked away, he called after her. "You escaped this time, but we'll finish this later."

The words slid over her like a threat, and she hurried to find Zach or Jake's buffering presence.

\*\*\*\*

After close that night, Sharlie sat in her office entering numbers into her computer. Her fingers flew over the keys.

She jumped when someone cleared his throat.

Logan stood in front of her desk. She'd been so involved she hadn't heard him walk in.

He grinned. "Sorry," he said, not looking sorry at all. "I didn't mean to startle you. I thought we could finish that conversation now."

"I don't think so. I have a lot to do, and I'm tired. I want to go home and get in bed." The minute the words were out of her mouth, she wished she hadn't uttered them. Logan's gaze darkened. For a moment, she stared at the familiar gleam in his eyes. How many countless times had he looked at her in the same way?

He had no right to look at her like that now.

She turned away, pretending sudden interest in the glowing computer screen. Something caught her eye in the bank of numbers there. "I've got to check on something in the store room." She rose and walked around Logan to the door.

"You're always running away from me. Why is that?" His quiet words stopped her.

She denied the truth in them. "I'm not running away. I have things to do." She turned in the doorway. "Good night."

Instead of taking the hint, Logan followed her down the hall and into the tiny room. She stifled a groan. Didn't the man ever give up?

"I want to talk to you about yesterday." He reached for the doorknob.

"No! Don't," Sharlie cried, but it was too late. Logan had closed the door behind him.

"What's the matter?"

She pushed past him in the small space, ignoring the brush of his body against hers. She grasped the door handle, knowing it was useless. "Damn."

"What's going on?"

"We're locked in." She whirled to face Logan.

"That's impossible. This door shouldn't lock from the inside." He reached around her to try the door.

She shrank away from his accidental touch and glared at him. "It's broken. We're locked in. We'll have to yell for help. Pete can open the door from the outside."

Logan shook his head. "Pete left."

"What? What about Zach or Jake?"

"Nope," Logan said. "Everyone left. I told Pete I wanted to finish something up, and he didn't have to stick around."

Sharlie looked at him in dismay, then brightened. "Do you have your cell phone?"

"Yeah," Logan began.

"Great. Then we can call—"

"Upstairs in the office."

"We're going to be stuck in here all night." She turned away to pace the small, confined area. The tiny space only allowed for three or four steps before she had to turn and change direction. Each time her steps took her near Logan, the spicy scent of his aftershave washed over her.

"What time does someone come in the morning?" Logan asked.

"Morning?" She tossed an angry look over her shoulder. "We finished a workday at," she glanced at her watch, "three a.m. Try afternoon. Probably about two or three."

"You're kidding."

"Logan," she explained with forced patience. "This is a bar. We work at night, almost all night. Then we sleep in the next day."

Logan shrugged, then rearranged a stack of boxes, and sat down.

"What are you doing?"

"Making myself comfortable. It sounds like we're going to be here a while."

Sharlie stared at him. No way in hell was she going to spend the night with Logan in the storeroom. Not after the way he'd kissed her at the rodeo. "We have to get out of here."

"We will at—what did you say?—two or three."

"How can you be so calm about this?"

"Relax," Logan said. "It's not my first choice for

a place to spend the night, but it's not the end of the world. We won't be locked in forever."

No, it'd only seem like an eternity. "I can't spend the night here with you," she blurted.

Logan rose, sudden fury in his eyes. "That's it, isn't it? It's not that you mind spending the night here. It's that you have to spend it with me. You wouldn't be so upset if you were locked in here with Zach." The angry words echoed in the confined space.

"Zach has nothing to do with it," Sharlie snapped.

"Then what's the problem?" Logan took a step toward her.

She stepped backwards to avoid his approach and stumbled over a box.

Logan's strong arm encircled her waist, preventing her from falling. Sharlie caught her breath as her body pressed against him. She raised her eyes to his.

The anger in his eyes had turned to awareness. His breath hitched. The temperature in the tiny room rose.

Logan's gaze roamed every inch of her face, finally coming to rest on her lips.

Her pulse quickened, the beat thundering in her ears. They were so close she could feel the cadence of his heart. She sucked in a gasp of air.

His gaze met hers again. "I've tried to stop thinking about you like this. But I can't."

Sharlie licked dry lips, then cursed inwardly when the action drew his attention there once more. His head lowered.

"Don't," she managed.

"Don't what?" Logan's warm breath caressed her cheek.

"Don't kiss me."

"Why not?"

"Because I don't want you to." Even to her own ears the protest sounded weak.

"Liar," Logan taunted.

"Please," she tried one last time, shaking her head in a vain attempt to deny the feelings coursing through her.

Logan cupped the back of her head, stilling the motion. "I have to." His words melted into a kiss as their lips met.

The gentle insistence of his mouth coaxed a response from her. Her lips parted of their own accord, allowing the kiss to deepen. Their breath mingled. The moist heat threatened to make her knees buckle.

"Don't you remember?" Logan's husky voice whispered, as his lips left hers to trail down the column of her throat. "Remember how good it was," he murmured before his mouth captured hers once again.

Half-forgotten feelings assaulted Sharlie as his tongue slid past her parted lips. Her knees gave, and he wrapped her in his embrace, drawing her even closer. Her breasts nestled against the firm muscles in his chest. She felt every breath he took.

Fighting to hold on to her sanity, she forced herself to remember.

How he'd left her.

She found the strength to pull away. "No."

"No?" Logan's breathing was erratic.

She struggled to get her emotions under control. "I won't let this happen again."

"What's wrong with this happening?" His words were harsh with desire.

"You can't expect to walk back into my life and pick up where we left off. Too much has changed. You don't belong here."

A shadow of pain flickered in Logan's eyes, but the emotion was so fleeting Sharlie wondered if she'd imagined it. He turned from her and ran his fingers through his raven hair. When he faced her again, his expression was clear. He sat down on the makeshift chair of boxes. "I'm going to get some shut eye." He leaned his head against the wall and lowered his lids.

Sharlie stood in the center of the storeroom feeling awkward. Aftershocks from his kiss shot through her body. Her knees were rubbery, and her hand trembled as she pushed back a lock of hair from her forehead. She slid down on the hard floor, resting her back against a stack of boxes.

She had known it would be difficult dealing with Logan now that he was back in town. She hadn't realized how difficult. Everything he did or said brought back memories of the past. Some bittersweet, some painful. What would it be like if he hadn't left?

They'd be a family.

Logan had always wanted a big family. He knew what it was like to live without a father. Their single parent households had been one of the first things they'd realized they had in common. Her mother had died when Sharlie was a little girl, and Logan had never known his father. He had vowed time and again that his kids would never have to experience the things he had been through growing up.

She'd robbed him of the chance to get to know his own child. He'd never forgive her for that. She glanced at his sleeping form, watching the slow rise and fall of his chest as he breathed steadily now. She would give anything to fall asleep next to him every night, safe and secure in his sheltering arms. The past wouldn't matter. Their baby wouldn't be gone.

She pulled her knees up and hugged them to her chest. She lowered her head. Afternoon was a long time away.

****

The click of the door woke Sharlie. Zach and Pete practically tumbled into the storeroom. Zach came to an abrupt halt, a strange look on his face.

Only then did she realize she was nestled against Logan. His arm was around her shoulders, and her head rested on his chest. At some point he'd joined her on the floor.

She extricated herself from their intimate position and scrambled to her feet. She threw her arms around Pete. "How did you know we were in here?"

Pete glanced at Logan, a slight frown on his face. "We saw your cars in the lot where you'd left them last night. Nothing was shut down in the bar, so we figured you were still here. We were mighty worried for a while."

Zach, who had remained silent up until now, spoke up. "I remembered you mentioned checking some inventory in here, and I knew this lock hadn't been fixed yet." He grabbed her arms when she moved from Pete's embrace. "Are you okay?" The look he tossed at Logan was unmistakable.

"I'm fine."

"We sure are glad to see you guys," Logan added.

"How long were you in here?" Zach asked.

Sharlie shrugged. "I don't know, but it seemed like forever." She caught Logan's gaze, then looked away.

An uncomfortable silence settled over the group. Zach inched closer to her, and Logan's eyes narrowed at the movement.

"Well, I'm sure you two want to head home for a bit," Pete finally said. He led the way out of the tiny room. "I suppose you're going to charge me overtime for this," he joked.

Everyone laughed, easing the tension.

"I want to get out of these clothes," Sharlie said

to Pete. "I'll be back in a bit."

"No rush, honey. We'll hold down the fort here until you get back."

"I won't be long."

"I'll walk you to your car," Zach said, casting another glance at Logan.

"I'm going to head out for a change of clothes myself." Logan stepped in front of her and raised her hand to his lips, kissing the back of it. But the calculating look in his eyes didn't match the old-fashioned gesture. "It was a pleasure being locked in the storeroom with you, Miss Sharlie."

His meaning was clear, and Sharlie felt Zach tense behind her. She glared at Logan.

"See you gentlemen later."

"What the hell was that supposed to mean?"

Sharlie watched Logan stride away before turning to face Zach.

"Now, Zach. I'm sure Logan didn't mean anything by his comment," Pete said.

Zach's angry gaze didn't leave hers. "What happened in the storeroom?"

Warm, moist lips sprang to mind. Deep sensual kisses that left her weak from the memory. She could still feel the hard strength of Logan's body pressed against her. "Nothing happened," she lied.

Then she changed the subject because she couldn't bear to think about it any longer. "I need to go home for a while before the dance tonight. I'll see you later, okay?"

"Sharlie?"

But she hurried out the door. Away from The Corral. Away from Zach's probing questions. Away from the memory of Logan's kiss.

Chapter Four

Later, Sharlie raced into The Corral, almost colliding with Pete.

"Whoa there, honey," he cried, grabbing her arms to steady her. "Where's the fire?"

"I'm so sorry I'm late," she panted, trying to catch her breath.

Pete looked at his watch and raised an eyebrow. "Five minutes? You're this wound up over five minutes?"

Calmer now, Sharlie shrugged. "I don't want to miss the rodeo dance. This is a big night." Each year The Corral closed its doors to outsiders, permitting only the rodeo participants and their guests in for the final night the rodeo was in town. The tradition had been around as long as the event itself.

Pete chuckled. "I've got to admit this is one of my favorite parts of Rodeo Week. But don't you go worrying about this place. Plenty of people are around to make sure things run okay. Zach's on tonight, and Logan is downstairs keeping an eye on things."

Sharlie grimaced at the mention of Logan's name. "He's back already?" She had wanted to arrive before he did. "He's made himself at home here, hasn't he?"

"Yes, he has. And that's what I wanted him to do." Pete paused, then continued, his tone cautious. "I heard what you told Zach, but did something happen between you and Logan in the storeroom?"

The concern in Pete's eyes almost undid her. The temptation to tell him everything overcame her.

41

It would feel so good to not carry the burden by herself anymore. But she wouldn't saddle Pete with the mistakes she'd made. He'd already done enough for her.

"Nothing happened," she said.

Pete studied her a moment, then nodded. "I wish you felt better about Logan buying this place."

Feel good about Logan buying the bar? That would be the day. She didn't want to analyze her feelings about Logan. On the one hand she hated him for leaving her all those years ago, running away with a sizeable check in his pocket. Trouble was, the other hand, not to mention the rest of her body, tingled and grew warm at the memory of his kisses. And that was even more dangerous, because nothing could ever happen between them again.

She shook her head in an attempt to clear it of troubling thoughts, then turned her attention back to Pete. "I..." she faltered, trying to find the words to reassure him.

"Never mind, sweetheart. Things will all work out fine." They descended the stairs leading down to the bar. "Why were you late?"

"My darn car wouldn't start."

"Again?" Pete's face once again reflected his concern. "Didn't I tell you to have it looked at?"

Sharlie smiled, warmed by the note of parental concern in Pete's voice. "You did, and I will. I promise. Scouts honor." She made a cross motion over her heart.

"If it's a question of money, I can loan you—"

"Forget it, Pete. I can take care of myself."

"I know you can, honey." He gave her shoulders an affectionate squeeze. "I didn't mean to upset you."

"I appreciate the offer, but I'm fine. I haven't gotten around to taking my car to the shop." She hoped she sounded convincing. Money was tight, and she couldn't spare the amount it would take to fix her old car up.

"Okay, I'll let you be. Remember to relax and have some fun yourself tonight."

"I will." Sharlie grinned at the retreating back of her boss. Her smile remained to greet Zach as he strolled over. "Hey, cowboy."

"Evenin', darlin'," Zach answered, touching the brim of his straw hat in a jaunty greeting.

Relief filled her when he made no mention of what had happened earlier. "Any action yet tonight?"

"Nope. Of course you'd know that if you'd show up on time, boss lady." Zach cuffed her on the arm.

She glared up at him. "My darn car wouldn't start."

Zach's teasing look changed to one of disapproval. "I thought you were going to have that junk heap you call a car looked at."

"Don't start, Zach," she warned. "I already got a lecture from Pete."

Zach threw up his hands in mock surrender. "All right, I give up. Anyway, I have to get back to work. Keep an eye on things around here."

"Keep an eye on those pretty barrel racers you mean," Sharlie teased, seeing the direction his eyes had wandered.

Zach grinned. "It's a tough job, but somebody's got to do it."

She laughed as he sauntered away, but the laughter died in her throat as her glance collided with Logan's across the room. He was watching her with that hard look in his eyes again. She turned away from his penetrating stare and looked at the dance floor.

Colorful skirts flared out, brushing against soft, worn denim as couples twirled across the parquet floor. Her booted foot tapped in time to the pulsing rhythm of the live band's music. Her own skirt swayed against her bare legs. She had opted against her usual jeans for this special night.

"Care to dance, ma'am?" A husky voice drawled in her ear.

Sharlie's quick refusal turned into a smile of acceptance when she saw Jake standing behind her. "Are you sure Janet won't mind?" she asked, teasing him as she placed her hand in his.

"Nah," Jake responded with a grin, leading her to the dance floor. "Besides, she's dancing with Pete." He nodded at the mismatched couple across the floor.

The night slipped away as she went from one partner to another, alternating dancing with periodic walks around the bar to make sure things were all in order. The opportunity to relax and let go a little felt wonderful. The annual dance was a welcome break from the everyday routine of The Corral. She had vowed to ignore Logan, but she couldn't keep from watching him moving across the dance floor with various partners throughout the night.

As her gaze met his, Sharlie wrenched her eyes away from the sight of him holding the curvaceous Rodeo Queen in his arms for a Stationary Cha-Cha. The heavily make-upped pageant winner pressed her bottom into the cradle of Logan's thighs as they executed the sensual rolling hip movement that began the dance. Sharlie swallowed, her throat dry.

Catching her glance again as the partners turned in the rhythmic dance Logan had the audacity to wink. She missed a step and stumbled, feeling Zach catch her close against him.

"Sorry," she murmured.

"No problem," Zach replied, before releasing her back into the usual dance position after one too many heartbeats.

Sharlie cursed to herself. When the song ended,

she stepped out of Zach's arms. "I need to check on things," she offered as an excuse. She made her way off the floor, pushing through the couples crowded around.

Before she could escape, her arm was grasped from behind. She turned to find Logan standing far too close for comfort.

"Would you care to dance?"

"Sorry, I have to get back to work." She tried to remove her arm from his gentle, yet firm grip.

Logan cast a cursory glance around the room. "Things look fine. Everything's under control."

Once again, she attempted to free herself without making a scene. "Please let go. I have work to do. I'm busy."

Logan's grip tightened, his eyes darkening as he gazed down at her. "You weren't too busy to dance with Zach, or Jake, or about a dozen other cowboys tonight."

"I didn't notice you lacking any partners yourself," Sharlie retorted, then bit her tongue when a knowing grin appeared on his face.

"Jealous?" Logan taunted.

"Hardly. I need to get back to work."

"You work for me now."

"Not yet," she muttered.

"Close enough." He swept her into the steps of the dance before she could protest again.

The fast rhythm prevented Sharlie from speaking as she concentrated on keeping up with the pace of the dance. Expecting to be released at the conclusion of the song, she was dismayed when the band began a smooth waltz, and Logan pulled her closer. Less than an arm's length separated them, and she could feel the heat emanating from him. Her traitorous body warmed, more from contact with the man holding her than from exertion. She couldn't get away without causing a scene, so she continued to dance, glaring at Logan from under her lashes.

"Didn't your mama ever tell you that your face will freeze like that?"

"Didn't your mama ever tell you it isn't polite to dance with an unwilling partner?"

Logan threw back his head and laughed. Nearby couples turned to look at the pair.

"I'm glad you find this amusing," Sharlie said, aggravated that so many people were seeing her dance with Logan. She didn't want to be associated with him in any way.

The waltz ended, but her attempt to leave was once again thwarted when Logan didn't release her. Her unease grew when the band announced its last dance, a slow ballad. A sigh of relief escaped when Zach approached from the far side of the dance floor. Even encouraging Zach with a slow dance was better than being held by Logan any longer.

As Zach finally reached them and opened his mouth to speak, Logan cut him off. "Sorry, this dance is mine." He turned Sharlie away from the bouncer and pulled her against him.

Their bodies touched from chest to thigh. His hard strength cradled her soft curves. The muscles in his legs flexed and relaxed as he shuffled to the slow strains of the dance. The heat of him penetrated through the thin protection of their clothing and burned into Sharlie. At the memory of his kisses, her heart rate accelerated.

Anger followed as she remembered the cruelty of his words.

She distanced her body from his in the scant millimeters his embrace would allow and shot him a quelling look. "That was rude."

Logan shrugged. "He'll get over it."

Sharlie inhaled as his muscular chest rose and brushed against her breasts. His eyes darkened as their gazes caught and held for several heartbeats.

Her breath hitched as he inclined his head and kissed her behind the ear. She forgot to breathe altogether when the warm moistness of his tongue touched the pulse that fluttered there before he lifted his head.

Drawing in air on a soft gasp, Sharlie hissed, "Stop it."

"No one's watching."

"I don't want you to do that."

"Liar," Logan said, his eyes glittering.

"Please, don't," she whispered as his head dipped toward her, his gaze focused on her lips.

Before her body could betray her, the song ended, and Logan released her. Without a backward glance, Sharlie hurried off the floor. She had almost reached her office when Zach stopped her.

"What was that all about?"

Hearing the combination of anger and hurt in his tone, Sharlie bit off a sigh. She wasn't in the mood to deal with Zach's jealousy.

"Nothing. I'm sorry Logan was rude to you, Zach."

"Is there something going on between you two? Do you like that guy?"

Did she like Logan? She wasn't sure how she felt about him any more, but she was sure that the word *like* wasn't strong enough to describe any feelings she'd ever had for him. "Nothing's going on between Logan and me."

Zach made no comment, but his disgruntled expression didn't relax at all.

She sighed again, but her tone was soft. "Look. I knew Logan a long time ago. Ages ago."

"Is that why he keeps hanging around here all the time? Because of you?"

"No, he's not here because of me."

"Then why is he here all the time?"

Sharlie hedged. She couldn't reveal anything

else to Zach without breaking her promise to Pete. "Please believe me. It's not what you think."

She could tell Zach wasn't satisfied, but he didn't ask any further questions.

"I have a ton of work to finish before I leave tonight, so I'd best get started." She inched closer to her office door.

"I'll wait and walk you out. Do you need a ride home?"

"No, I got my car started. I'm going to be here for a while, why don't you go on ahead."

"You sure?"

"I'm sure." She laid her hand on his arm. "I'll be fine. I'll see you tomorrow."

"Okay, I'll see you tomorrow, darlin'." He touched the tip of his finger to her nose, winked, and walked away.

She leaned her head against the wall and closed her eyes. Zach needed to find someone soon. The quicker, the better.

"I see you've kissed and made up with your cowboy."

Her eyes flew open at Logan's words. His cold tone matched the ice in the depths of his gaze.

"I won't discuss Zach with you. I told you before. It's none of your business." She turned and walked into her office. "If you'll excuse me, I have work to do." She closed the door, putting an end to their discussion and shielding herself from his glare.

****

An hour later Sharlie stretched, stifling a yawn as she glanced at the clock. She groaned, then switched off her computer, grabbed her purse, and locked her office door.

As she made her way through the darkened hallway toward the front door, visions of an old ghost town came to mind. A light burned in Pete's office, so she stopped to say good-night.

Her words faltered when she saw Logan seated behind the desk. He looked up. They stared at one another until she broke the silence. "Well, I'm done for the night."

Logan looked behind her. "What, no Zach waiting gallantly to take you home?"

"Why do you have such a problem with Zach?" Sharlie held up a hand. "Never mind. I'm too tired to deal with this tonight." She turned to go.

"Wait." Logan stood and walked around the desk. "I'll walk you out."

"Don't bother."

Logan switched off the lights and closed the office door, then followed her out into the hallway. "I insist."

"Suit yourself."

They walked to the parking lot without speaking. The stillness of the night pressed down on her, smothering her with its oppressiveness. Gravel crunched beneath their feet in the gaping silence. Sharlie opened her car door and slid behind the wheel. Before she could close the door, Logan grabbed it.

"Sharlie?"

In the dim glow of the parking lot lights, she studied him. The lines bracketing his eyes and mouth were deeper than she remembered. "What?"

His gaze searched hers, but then he shook his head. "Never mind. Good night." He shut her door and stepped back from the car.

She shrugged and inserted the key into the ignition. Nothing happened when she turned it. She cursed and tried again. She smacked the steering wheel with both hands. "Damn."

Logan opened the door and frowned. "What's the matter?"

"My darn car won't start. This happened earlier. It's why I was late for work."

"Scoot over, let me try."

She slid across the seat. He got in, then pushed the seat back to accommodate his long legs. He turned the key.

"Sounds like the battery is dead. Or it could be the alternator."

Sharlie wasn't sure what kind of repair that would entail, but bet it would be expensive. Leaning her head against the back of the seat, she groaned.

"This happened before?"

"I've been having some trouble with my car."

"Why didn't you have it looked at?"

"I never got around to it," Sharlie lied. No way in the world would she tell him she couldn't afford the repair bill.

"I'll call a tow truck."

"Can't you jump it or something?"

"That won't fix the problem. You'll have the same trouble tomorrow. We'll have it towed to the nearest station, and they can fix it for good. You should have it back in a couple of days." Logan paused. "Is that what you're worried about, getting to work for a couple of days?"

"No," Sharlie replied. "Zach can pick me up."

The air in the small car crackled.

"Of course. Good ol' Zach to the rescue."

"Are you going to start that again?"

Logan looked at her. "No," he said at last. "I'm not. Come on, I'll call a tow truck and give you a ride home."

Sharlie wanted to refuse, but her options were limited. She followed Logan to his truck.

"Do you use a particular garage?" he asked, retrieving a cell phone from the glove compartment.

Sharlie shook her head.

"Is Dave's still in business?"

"I think so." The mention of the auto shop brought a sweet memory of the past. Logan had worked there during high school. She had spent countless hours waiting for him to finish his shift so they could spend time together.

After making the call, Logan turned to her. "Now let's get you home. Which way?"

They rode in more or less companionable silence. She directed him as needed, until they pulled into the parking lot of her apartment complex.

Logan cut the engine and stared at the peeling paint on the façade.

"Not quite the Montgomery mansion is it?" His tone was neutral, but his eyes were filled with questions.

Questions she didn't want to answer.

She turned away, groping for the door handle in the darkened interior of the truck. "Thanks for the ride home."

Logan was already out of the vehicle and at her side when she stepped down off the high seat. "I'll walk you to your door."

"Don't bother. It's late. I'm sure you want to be getting home."

He grasped her elbow. "Humor me." He guided her into the building and waited while she unlocked the inner door.

"See, I'm in. Thanks." She started to close the heavy door, but Logan's hand stopped her.

"Could I get a glass of water for the road?"

What was he up to? Against her better judgment, she opened the door wider.

Logan followed her down the dim hallway, waiting while she unlocked the bolts on her apartment door. Her fingers trembled, and she fumbled with the keys.

"Here, let me." With a smooth motion he removed them from her hand and unlocked the door, stepping aside to allow her to enter.

His take-charge manner grated on her nerves,

but she accepted her keys without comment and headed for the kitchen, switching on lights as she went. His presence dominated her tiny apartment. She wanted to give him his glass of water and send him on his way. Before he could ask any of the questions lurking in his eyes.

She returned to the living room. "Here you go."

Logan sprawled on her couch, his black cowboy hat discarded on the coffee table. The hat no doubt cost more than the table. He ran his fingers through the dark strands of his hair. The action carried a poignant reminder of the past.

"Thanks." Logan reached for the glass she held out.

His fingers brushed hers, and Sharlie yanked her hand away.

Logan sipped his water and looked around the living room. Sharlie looked, too, trying to see the worn furniture and secondhand tables through his eyes.

This time the questions in his eyes were veiled when he turned to her. She stood watching him, feeling out of place in her own apartment, while he had clearly made himself at home.

"Nice place," he finally said.

"I like it." She couldn't help the defensive note that crept into her voice.

Logan raised an eyebrow.

Sharlie looked pointedly at the clock on the wall. "It's getting late."

Logan drained his glass and placed it on a coaster, then rose to his feet.

She walked him to the door. "Thanks again for driving me home."

"No problem. I'm glad I was there to help."

Their strained arguments of the past few weeks had evolved into inane small talk, at least for now. Soon they'd be talking about the weather.

"Do you need a ride to work tomorrow?"

Sharlie shook her head, "No, I'll call— someone."

For a moment Logan's eyes darkened, but then he hid the emotion. "All right." He lifted his hand, as if to touch her, but dropped it before making contact. "Good night, Sharlie."

She closed the door, then listened to the steady tread of his boots as he made his way down the hall. The outer door closed with a soft thud. He was gone.

Sharlie leaned against the door. Her skin tingled from his near touch. Logan had taken over her apartment in the few minutes he'd been there. His hat lay forgotten on her coffee table, resting near his empty water glass. The cushions of the couch still bore the impression of his body, and the spicy smell of his aftershave lingered in the air, teasing her.

She plumped the cushions back into shape, then washed and dried the glass, putting it out of sight on the top shelf of the cabinet. The hat she placed on the table by the door as a reminder to bring it to work tomorrow.

Satisfied with her hasty repair work, she switched off the lights and headed to bed. As she lay there, trying to fall asleep, she wished she could clean Logan out of her thoughts as easily as she had straightened the apartment. He was an enigma to her. One minute he was ranting mad, the next he was tenderly concerned. She didn't want to— couldn't—deal with the caring side of him. It brought back far too many memories. Worse, it made her crave things she couldn't have.

Being angry with him was far easier. Anger and regret had dominated her thoughts of him for the past twelve years. Without anger would she be able to keep hiding her guilty secret? If Logan ever found out what she'd done to their child, there'd be hell to pay.

Chapter Five

"Please sign here, Mr. Reed."

Logan penned his name on the line indicated by the real estate agent, then sat back to survey the interior of the spacious ranch house he'd purchased. His mind filled, however, with the image of Sharlie's small apartment, rather than the large family room visible from the pass-through in the kitchen. She was the daughter of one of the richest men in the county. Why was she living in such meager conditions? Years ago it had been him living in a small apartment, while Sharlie dwelled in the lap of luxury. What had happened to change all that?

"Well, that should do it." The real estate agent rose from the stool next to Logan's and held out her hand.

Logan stood and grasped it in a brief handshake, noting that although the woman was attractive her touch didn't cause his pulse to race. The mere thought of Sharlie caused his breath to quicken.

"The copies on the table are yours," the agent continued. She gathered the remaining papers and stuffed them into a legal sized folder. She looked at Logan. "If there's anything else you need," her throaty voice held an unmistakable invitation, "give me a call."

Ignoring the double entendre in her words, he escorted her to the wide doors leading to the front porch of the house. "I think that's it for now. I'll let you know when I'm ready for those papers on The Corral."

Looking a bit disappointed, the woman made her way down the porch steps, her slim skirt and high spiked heels impeding her progress.

Logan couldn't help comparing the long legs revealed by the short skirt with Sharlie's legs encased in tall cowboy boots, topped with a full, sexy skirt that swung against her thighs with every movement. The sight had almost driven him wild the night before. He groaned aloud at the memory. He knew the slow dance had been a mistake, but he had wanted, no *needed*, to feel her pressed against him. He'd thought of nothing else since kissing her.

He waved the agent off as she got into her car and drove down the gravel driveway, then he went back into the house. He was a homeowner now.

He took a long look around the family room. Things were coming along rather well. Except for one thing. He hadn't counted on Sharlie. At least not at this stage. He'd wanted to have everything in place before confronting her with the proof that he didn't need her or her father's money. He had his own money now.

In fact, it seemed as though he had more money than she did. He wondered again what had happened between her and her father. He presumed Montgomery didn't know about her living in the conditions she was, driving a car that had one wheel in the junkyard.

Which reminded him. He needed to make sure she made it to work. He pulled his cell phone from his pocket and dialed a number he somehow knew by heart.

****

Sharlie was almost finished with her make-up when the phone rang. Figuring Zach was calling to make sure she was ready, she answered without bothering to say hello.

"Hi, Zach. I'm almost ready. I'll be set by the

time you get here."

Silence greeted her. A silence that somehow felt angry.

"Zach?"

"It's not Zach."

"Logan?"

"Sorry to disappoint you." Even through phone wires the chill in his voice sent a shiver down her spine.

"I'm sorry, I—"

Logan cut off the apology. "I was calling to make sure you had a ride to work."

"Zach is going to—"

"So I gathered." His curt reply cut her off once again. "Well, we don't want to keep Zach waiting. See you at work."

"Logan?" The dial tone buzzed in her ear. He had severed the connection.

"Damn." She hung up the phone. Why did Logan act so angry at the mere mention of Zach's name?

If she was with Zach, what concern of Logan's was that? *He* had walked out on her. What she did with her life was none of his business. Her life with him was in the past, even if it had felt like coming home to be held in his arms.

The apartment building buzzer interrupted her wandering musings. She pressed the button on the speaker. "Yes?"

"It's me." Zach's disembodied voice filtered through the tiny speaker near the door.

"Come on in." She depressed the button to unlock the front entrance.

"I'm almost ready," she called over her shoulder, heading toward the bathroom, as Zach walked into her apartment.

"Take your time. We're early."

She returned to the living room a few minutes later. "Okay. I'm all set."

"Finally," Zach teased, rising from the couch.

She noted that having Zach sit on her couch wasn't nearly as unsettling as having Logan sitting there. Then again, everything Logan did these days had an unsettling effect on her. "Yeah, whatever."

"So what's up with your car—what's that?" The light tone of Zach's voice had faded, replaced with a hard edge.

She turned. "What's what?"

Zach's gaze was resting on Logan's hat, which lay on the table by the door.

"Oh, Logan left his hat here last night after—"

"What the hell was he doing here?"

Taken aback by the force of the anger simmering in Zach's voice, Sharlie became defensive. "He drove me home when my car wouldn't start."

"Why didn't you call me? I would have come and gotten you."

"At three in the morning?" What was with angry cowboys today?

"Do you even know this guy well enough to be accepting rides from him? Why did you let him in your apartment?"

"Look, Zach, Logan isn't a stranger. I told you. I knew him a long time ago. I'm perfectly safe with him." At least that was true unless Logan found out about the baby. Nothing would save her from his wrath then.

The short ride to The Corral was strained. Sharlie could still feel the undercurrents of Zach's anger, and she was in no mood to deal with Logan's glowering expression when she walked into the bar with the bouncer at her side.

The two men glared at each other until Logan muttered something about needing to make a phone call and stalked off.

****

The implications of that phone call made

themselves clear later that afternoon. Sharlie slammed down her own phone and marched into Logan's office. "What the hell do you think you're doing?"

Logan finished reading the papers in front of him, then leaned back in his chair. His gaze met hers. "I'm going over some old reports."

"That's not what I meant, and you know it." Sharlie nearly spit the words in his face. "How dare you."

"I dared," Logan replied. He made no pretense of misunderstanding her.

"Who do you think you are?"

"I was helping out a friend."

"We're not friends, Logan." They'd been much, much more. "I don't want your charity."

"Helping you pay for your car repairs isn't charity. And what do you mean we're not friends? I remember a time when we were very friendly."

She ignored the heat in Logan's eyes and did her best to ignore the answering flame that flared in the pit of her stomach. She remembered those times only too well.

Pushing thoughts of the past from her mind, she once again addressed the issue at hand. "I can take care of myself."

"No one said you couldn't."

"I don't need you to pay for my car."

"The guy at Dave's said you were going to leave the car until next week when you had the money."

Sharlie bit her lip. She'd have to have a talk with Dave about his employees. Didn't anyone know the meaning of discretion anymore? "So what?"

"So this way you can have it back sooner. Then you won't have to depend on anyone else to take you to work."

Realization dawned on her. Logan didn't want her riding to and from work with Zach every day.

"You had no right to call Dave's." She ignored Logan's shrug and repeated, "I'll take care of the situation myself."

"When?"

"That's no concern of yours. Stay out of it. Why do you care so much about my car anyway?" She glared at him, hands on her hips.

"Like I said, I hate to see you depending on other people to get you to and from this place. I was doing you a favor."

"I don't need you to do me any favors. And," she added, "it's no trouble getting a ride to work."

"Of course not. Good ol' Zach. His favors are okay, but mine aren't, is that it?"

Sharlie sighed. She got the feeling they weren't talking about her car any more. Life had been so much simpler before Logan had walked back into it. "What are you doing here?"

"Excuse me?" Logan's voice sounded perplexed at the abrupt change in conversation.

"Why did you come back?"

Logan shrugged again, but his careful tone and shuttered eyes belied the casual gesture. "I wanted a permanent place to set up my rodeo camp."

"Why here?"

"I had some fond memories of this place. And this is a rodeo town." He paused, then looked at her for a moment. "Why couldn't you get the money for your car from your father?"

Sharlie disliked the feeling of having the tables turned on her. She had been the one asking the questions. Considering her reply, she sank into one of the chairs facing Logan's desk. She twirled a strand of hair around her finger and studied him. She heard no censure in his tone, and his eyes reflected the serious nature of his question.

"We don't talk anymore," she replied, wondering why she felt compelled to answer him.

"Why?"

"We had a falling out. A difference of opinion."

"When?"

Her eyes met Logan's gaze without wavering. "About twelve years ago."

Logan drew in his breath.

"That's right." Her voice rose. "Right after you left."

The words hung in the air, heavy in the silence.

"Sharlie, I—"

She pushed out of her chair and headed for the door. "Are you still planning on buying this place?"

"Yes."

"Isn't it funny how you can do anything when you have money? And isn't it ironic that you're the one with all the money now? Strange, isn't it?"

Logan made no reply to her string of questions, but then again, she didn't expect one. She did notice, however, that a muscle worked in his jaw.

She paused, her hand on the doorknob. "I'll take care of the car myself."

"Too late. It's already done."

"Then undo it. I won't be indebted to you." Sharlie closed the office door behind her.

****

The next day Sharlie was chatting with Pete in his office when Logan poked his head in.

"Am I interrupting anything?"

Pete smiled in greeting. "Not at all, come on in."

Logan glanced at her, but spoke to Pete. "I had those preliminary papers drawn up on The Corral."

Sharlie caught her breath. The thing she'd dreaded most over the last few weeks was happening. Logan was buying The Corral. Her heart thudded painfully against her ribs.

"Great," Pete said, taking the papers from Logan and placing them on his desk.

"Do you have those financial recaps I wanted to

look at?"

"Sharlie will be able to get those for you."

"What?" She looked up at the sound of her name.

"I'd like you to go over the financial recaps with Logan. Answer any questions he might have."

Sharlie wanted to groan. Why was Pete always assigning her to work with Logan?

"That would be great," Logan said.

The knowing look in his eyes set her teeth on edge.

"Fine," she replied, a sweet smile on her face for Pete's sake. "They're in my office. I'll get them for you."

"Why don't we work in there?" Logan asked with an innocent look.

Sharlie glared at him. "Sure." The last thing she wanted to do was be alone with him. She wasn't able to think clearly when he was around. She couldn't imagine being confined in her tiny office with him all afternoon.

Logan made himself comfortable in one of the chairs facing her desk, while she rummaged in a file cabinet to find the desired papers. She pulled them from the drawer and tossed them on the desk. As she headed toward the door, Logan's hand on her wrist stopped her.

"Where are you going?"

"I figured I'd give you some privacy to look these over," she hedged, pulling her hand from his grasp. She quelled the urge to rub the spot that had warmed from his touch.

"Are you afraid of being alone with me?" Logan asked, his gaze shrewd.

"No," she denied, chagrined that he could read her so well after all these years.

"Then stay. I might have some questions."

"Fine." She resumed her seat behind the desk. "I

61

have some work to do anyway."

She switched on her computer and waited while the desired spreadsheet came up on the screen. As she input the requisition list, she was distracted by Logan's presence. His spicy aftershave enveloped her in intoxicating waves. The husky drawl of his voice when he asked a question skittered over her nerves. His masculinity overwhelmed her tiny office. Finally she couldn't stand it anymore. She had to escape.

"I'm going to get something to drink."

"Sounds great. Could you grab me a water?"

"Yeah, sure," she said with false politeness. She didn't want to do anything for him.

On her way back to the office, she ran into Kate, one of the waitresses who had come in early to set tables.

"Someone dropped this off for Logan. Pete said he was working with you."

Sharlie grabbed the thick manila envelope. "Thanks. I'll see that he gets it." She couldn't help noticing the return address label from a local real estate firm.

"Here, this came for you." She dropped the package into Logan's lap as she walked back into the office. His water glass landed on the desk with a sharp thud.

"I've been waiting for this," Logan said, opening the envelope and spreading the contents on her desk.

"Make yourself at home." Sarcasm laced her voice.

"Sorry," he said, not sounding sorry at all. "I want to take a look at these. They're the final papers on my house."

"You're buying a house, too?" Sharlie asked incredulously.

"You have a problem with that?" Logan's voice held a touch of irritation.

"You've done quite well for yourself since you left, haven't you?" With her father's money for a starter.

"As a matter of fact I have," Logan said, his tone controlled.

"I guess I shouldn't be surprised, now should I?" Sharlie's voice was bitter.

"No," Logan returned. "You shouldn't be." His gaze captured and held hers. "What did you think I'd do when I left here? Crawl under a rock and hide?"

"Of course not. All of that money would have gone to waste under a rock."

Logan's eyes turned to steel. "Let's get something straight right now."

Before he could finish, Pete walked into the office. "How's it going in here?"

Sharlie smiled brightly. "Fabulous," she lied.

"We were taking a break so I could look over the papers on the land I bought." Logan threw a mocking look at her.

"You'll need quite a spread if you want to stock it like you were saying for your camp," Pete said, falling into the vacant chair next to Logan.

"Yeah, this place should do the trick. The house itself is large, and there's plenty of land to set up camp and build a barn for the animals."

Sharlie continued working, trying to ignore the men's conversation. She didn't want to hear about Logan's plans for staying in town.

"This camp of yours sure is a great idea. What made you think of it?" Pete asked as he perused the specs in front of him.

"The rodeo caught my interest on a trip once. I guess it was in my blood from living here. And I've always loved kids. This was something I could do to combine the two."

"You planning on having any of your own? Kids that is."

Sharlie's heart squeezed painfully at Pete's innocent question.

"Yeah, I'd love to have a whole house full of them someday."

Sharlie choked on the water she'd sipped.

"Are you okay, honey?" Pete asked in concern.

Logan looked at her, curiosity in his eyes.

"I'm fine," she managed. "It went down the wrong way." Logan had always talked about having lots of kids. If it wasn't for her, he'd have at least one.

Not for the first time since he'd been back, she wondered why he hadn't married and started a family. She'd bet good money dozens of women out there would give their eyeteeth to be his wife and raise his children.

An ache blossomed in her heart and spread. Although she had ruined any chance of a future with Logan, she couldn't stand to think about him with another woman.

Pete rose from his chair. "Well, I'll let the two of you get back to work. Good luck with your house, Logan."

"Thanks. It feels good to be back home." He tossed Sharlie an enigmatic look. "I'm here to stay."

\*\*\*\*

Later that night, alone in her office at last, Sharlie breathed a sigh of relief. Her nerves were raw from dealing with Logan all day. After Pete had left, an uneasy truce had descended, and they had finished going over papers in more or less civil fashion.

Glancing down on her desk at the work schedule for the week, she grimaced at seeing Pete's attached note. He wanted her to give a copy of the schedule to Logan.

She couldn't deal with his presence much longer. Each day he got more and more involved at The

Corral. She had to find some way to change his mind about buying the bar. The guilt and pain she'd tried all these years to bury hovered too close to the surface with him around.

A knock on the door drew her gaze there. "Come on in, Kate," she said to the waitress who poked her head into the room. "What's up?"

"I need to have Wednesday off next week," Kate explained. "I already checked with one of the other girls, and she said she could trade with me. But I wanted to check with you first."

"I don't see why that should be a problem," Sharlie said, jotting a reminder onto the master schedule in front of her.

Pete's note caught her gaze once again. What if she didn't give Logan a copy of the schedule? He wouldn't be very effective in running the bar if he didn't know everything that was going on. Maybe Pete would see Logan wasn't the best person to sell The Corral to and find someone else to buy it.

## Chapter Six

"What the hell is going on here, Sharlie?" Logan's angry voice followed the crash of her office door against the wall.

Sharlie jumped, the pen in her fingers flying out of her grasp and onto the floor at Logan's feet. Her gaze followed its descent, then beginning at his boots, traveled up the length of his jean clad legs, over his flannel-shirted chest, and finally up to meet his smoldering eyes. She forced herself not to look away.

"It's time to stop playing games."

"Games?" she asked, trying to sound innocent. "What are you talking about?"

Logan held up a hand and began to tick things off on his fingers as he spoke. "Revised schedules that only I see. Waitstaff and bartending shifts that mysteriously don't match the lists I have. And let's not forget the cold shoulder I get from your ever-faithful bouncing duo."

"I had nothing to do with that. Zach and Jake must have formed their own opinions of you."

Logan's eyes darkened at the mention of Zach's name, but he made no comment.

Sharlie squirmed in her seat. She twisted a strand of hair around her finger and tried to direct her attention elsewhere. It proved to be impossible. Her thoughts had rarely been anywhere else except on Logan ever since he'd arrived back in town. As hard as she tried, she couldn't ignore his presence or forget his kisses. Every time she saw him, she remembered the feel of his mouth on hers.

That was dangerous. She couldn't get involved with Logan again. Even if by some miracle they were able to put the past behind them, she had no future to offer him. Not the kind he wanted.

He walked to her desk and flipped the calendar to an upcoming date. He thrust his finger at it, pointing. "Keep this date open."

"Why?"

"The bar will be closed for a private party."

"We don't close the bar for private parties. Anyone interested in having a large party is welcome to reserve the use of our banquet hall upstairs," Sharlie recited, as though talking to a customer.

"We'll be making an exception this time."

"Pete won't approve that."

"It's not Pete's decision to make anymore," Logan said quietly. "In fact, the bar will be closed so we can give him a proper good-bye party."

"What?" Sharlie felt as though the wind had been knocked out of her.

"You heard me, sweetheart. So you can tell all of your little friends to cut the crap. I know what you've been doing over these past few weeks. Trying everything in your power to get me to walk away from here. But it didn't work, did it?" Logan placed his hands on the edge of her desk and leaned over her. "I'm through with the Montgomerys trying to tell me what to do."

Sharlie jumped up, unable to stand him towering over her. "What the hell is that supposed to mean?"

"You're like your daddy, Sharlie." Ignoring her outraged gasp, Logan ruthlessly continued. "You think you can control everyone else's lives. But this time it won't work. You work for me now."

"Not any more. I quit."

"Not so fast."

Logan's words stopped her as she reached for the doorknob. "If you go, everyone goes."

"What?" She turned from the door to face him.

"That's right. Unless you stay, I fire everyone who's on staff right now. Including your beloved"— Logan's voice turned nasty—"Zach."

Sharlie gaped at him. "Why would you do that? You promised Pete you wouldn't change anything. I knew it. I told him from the beginning you would come in here and make all kinds of changes. How could you lie to him like that? Pete's a decent man."

"I didn't lie to Pete. As long as you stay on as the manager of this bar, things will stay the way they are right now. Well, except for the nonsense that's been going on lately."

"What do you care if I stay or not? Why would you want me to stay when I don't want to?"

For the first time since their battle of words began, Logan looked like he might be wounded, but the emotion was quick to disappear from his eyes. "Because for once I want to be the one in control."

"You keep saying that. What's with the control issues here?"

"Twelve years ago I left here under the Montgomery's control."

"And how convenient that turned out to be for you."

"Don't start with that again. I am not the guilty one here."

Logan's words zeroed in on her heart, setting it to pounding. No, he wasn't the one plagued by guilt. She alone carried that burden. Holding her breath, she waited, unable to respond.

Logan stared into her eyes, then frowned. "Why are you afraid of me, Sharlie? What are you hiding?"

She lowered her eyes. "I don't know what you mean."

"I think you do. I'm going to find out what it is."

He strode from the office.

The words hung in the air after Logan had closed the door behind him. Sharlie sank into a chair and lowered her head into the cradle of her arms on the desk. What was she going to do?

****

Later, alone in his house, Logan wondered when he was going to stop acting like a first class jerk around Sharlie. Their conversation haunted him. He had blackmailed her into staying, but the thought of never seeing her again bothered him more than he wanted to admit.

Turning on the shower, he adjusted the spray to a comfortable temperature. Nothing was going the way he had planned.

Her comment about being in control came back to him. She was right. He did have control issues. Ever since he'd left town he'd been determined to make it on his own without help from anyone. Growing up on the proverbial wrong side of the tracks had been hell. Back then he couldn't escape the circumstances of his life. As the only child of a single mother who barely could take care of herself, let alone a child, he'd always been dependent on others. Others who looked down on him because of where he lived.

Until he'd met Sharlie. It hadn't seemed to matter to her. At least not at first. In the end, she'd treated him like all the others.

While he'd been gone, his only goal in life had been to make enough money so people would respect him. From the start he'd wanted to be his own boss. The one in control.

He smiled grimly. How could Sharlie still know him so well?

He'd come back because he had so many things to prove to her—and her father. But her father didn't seem to be in the picture any more. Which was another puzzle.

Money didn't seem to matter to Sharlie. In fact, she seemed angry that he had money. Which didn't make any sense either.

Stripping off his clothes, he realized the only thing he was trying to prove now was that Sharlie didn't mean anything to him.

He wasn't doing a good job. He couldn't stay away from her. The memory of their kisses and the feel of her in his arms as they'd danced leaped into his mind. His body's involuntary reaction had him reaching to turn the faucet to cold.

After all this time he still wanted her.

He also wanted to know about the shadows lurking in those beautiful blue eyes of hers.

****

Pete walked into Sharlie's office early the following day. "I have a huge favor."

"Shoot, whatever you need," she answered with a smile.

"I need you to drive out to Logan's place and deliver something to him."

Her smile faded. "Out to Logan's?"

"I wouldn't ask, but I've got to stick around here for an appointment with my accountant. I need to have Logan look at these papers today."

"Isn't he coming in to the bar?"

"Not until later. He's workin' out at his new place, getting his camp set up. I think he's even got some kids coming by."

The image of Logan with the little girl in his arms at the rodeo flashed into Sharlie's mind, but she shook it away before she could dwell on it.

"Okay, I'll do it. But I'm only doing it for you."

"I know you are, and I appreciate it." Pete gave her an affectionate hug. "I hope you and Logan can come to some sort of understanding when he takes over. I'd hate the thought of leaving you here the way things are."

Sharlie smiled at her boss and friend. She'd
never tell him about Logan's emotional blackmail,
but it seemed the tension between her and Logan
hadn't gone unnoticed. Then again, how could
anyone not notice?

"Don't worry about us. Everything will be fine.
Where is this new place of Logan's?"

"It's the old Dawson place. Right over there off
of Route 22."

Sharlie's heart skipped a beat. She and Logan
had driven by that place hundreds of times during
high school. Dreaming about what it would be like to
live there together. To raise a family there.

The thought was nearly enough to stop her
heart all together. Pushing the disturbing thoughts
aside, she gave Pete a quick kiss on the cheek and
grabbed her keys and the papers. "Yeah, I know
where it is. I'll be back as soon as I can."

"Don't rush, honey. Take your time and enjoy
the drive. It's a beautiful day."

Sharlie took Pete's advice as she drove toward
Logan's new ranch. The vivid blue sky was dotted
with white clouds that looked like fluffy cotton balls
floating overhead. A warm breeze fluttered through
the open car window, scattering her hair. Colorful
leaves on the trees and the damp smell that lingered
in the air were signs that fall had arrived. She sang
along with the classic George Jones song on the
radio, trying to forget for a brief moment where she
was headed.

All too soon she pulled into the curved gravel
driveway in front of a sprawling ranch house. She
killed the engine, but sat in the car for a minute,
closing her heart to the pain of seeing the house of
her dreams. Once upon a time she had pictured
herself sitting on the wrap-around porch waiting for
Logan to return from work. She would have had

dinner on the stove. The kids would have been playing around back. The smallest would have been nestled in her arms. The thought of all the dreams that had been lost, of the heartbreaking decision she'd made, brought a familiar ache to her chest. Even after twelve years the pain hadn't dulled. Would the scars ever heal?

Before she could drive herself crazy, she threw open the car door and stepped out. Walking up the few steps to the double front doors, she studiously ignored the rocking chairs sitting in one corner of the porch. Receiving no reply to her knock, she called through the screen. "Logan?"

No answer. She remembered Pete mentioning that Logan would be working on his camp today. Maybe even have a client or two around.

Sharlie made her way down the steps and around the side of the house, her well worn boots crunching in the gravel. She stopped, dead in her tracks, as she walked right into a scene from her dreams. Or was it a nightmare?

Logan stood several yards away with a little girl no more than seven or eight years old. He held a rope in his hands and talked softly to the girl, who listened with rapt attention. Nodding, she took the rope, imitating the way Logan had been holding it.

Unnoticed, Sharlie watched, a lump the size of Texas in her throat, as Logan taught the girl, clad in miniature boots and a hat, how to hold the rope. With gentle care he guided her hands to the right spot on the rope, then stood back to let her throw. The procedure was repeated until at last the girl's throw made her mark, and he flashed her a thumbs-up accompanied by a grin. Even beneath the shadow from the brim of his hat, she could see the pride in his eyes as he smiled at the ecstatic girl.

Sharlie's eyes misted. If things had been different, she could be watching Logan teach his own daughter to rope. Tears blurring her vision, she turned to go, not caring if she delivered Pete's papers or not.

"Sharlie?" Logan's voice stopped her.

She couldn't face him until she'd regained her composure, so she kept her back to him, taking deep gulps of fresh air into her lungs.

"Sharlie?" His voice was nearer now.

She jumped when he touched her shoulder.

"Uh, hi." She turned to face him, but couldn't meet his eyes, not wanting him to see the trace of tears in her own.

"What are you doing here?"

"Pete asked me to bring these by." She held up the papers, hoping Logan couldn't see how her hand trembled. "He needs you to look at them today. I didn't mean to interrupt." She nodded toward the little girl still clutching the rope.

"You're not interrupting. Amy and I are about finished here."

Sharlie's heartbeat quickened at the light touch of Logan's hand on the small of her back. His hand felt like fire through the thin denim of her shirt as he led her toward the little girl.

"This is Amy. Amy, this is Sharlie. She's a friend of mine. Sharlie, this is Mrs. Fuller. Amy's mom."

Sharlie hadn't even noticed the petite woman sitting on a nearby split-rail fence.

"Nice to meet you." Mrs. Fuller shook Sharlie's hand, then inclined her head toward Logan. "This camp is a wonderful idea. Logan's great with kids."

Sharlie smiled to hide the hurt the woman's words caused. "Yeah, he is."

The woman turned to Logan. "Thanks again for the lesson. We'll be back next week. Let us know when you set up a permanent schedule. Amy would love to be part of your first group."

"Yeah, thanks, Mr. Reed." Amy gave Logan a

quick hug, then skipped after her mother around the side of the house.

Logan turned to Sharlie. "Why don't we take those papers into the house?" Before she could refuse, he led the way through the back screen door, which closed after them with a soft slam.

She found herself in a large kitchen equipped with modern appliances.

"Have a seat." Logan indicated the stools in front of the breakfast bar. "Can I get you something to drink?"

"No, thanks, I can't stay. I need to get back." She gritted her teeth at the inane pleasantries.

"If you can spare a few more minutes, I'll look these over and send them with you. Then Pete can have them back today."

Logan's fingers brushed hers as he took the papers from her hand. He made no comment, but raised one dark eyebrow when she flinched at the contact.

Damn. How unfair of him to use Pete to make her stay. She shrugged. "Sure, take your time."

"This won't take long. Are you sure you don't want something to drink?"

"I'm fine." She looked out over the large family room off the kitchen. The room was bare of furniture. Apparently Logan hadn't gotten that far yet. Was the rest of house empty as well? Where was Logan sleeping?

Restless, she wandered around the kitchen.

Logan looked up from the papers he was perusing. "Feel free to take a look around."

Although she knew it would be torture, Sharlie's curiosity got the best of her. "If you don't mind?"

"Go ahead. Make yourself at home."

She winced at his choice of words. She walked from the kitchen into the adjoining family room. A stone fireplace spanned the far wall, and the back of the house boasted a huge picture window that looked out over the acres of land belonging to the ranch. Far in the distance she could make out the shadowy shapes of the mountains. Opposite the window were the doors leading to the front porch. A hallway led to the bedrooms on the other side of the house.

She crossed to the hallway, her boots echoing on the hardwood floors, and peeked into each of the bedrooms. The master suite had another large window overlooking the back of the spread and a whirlpool tub in the bathroom. Sharlie averted her eyes from the air mattress and its tangled sheets on the floor. A second bathroom held a convenient place in the hallway between two of the other rooms.

Retracing her steps, she passed back through the family room and the kitchen to the formal living and dining room. A third picture window was the focal point of the living room.

She stood and stared out the window, not really noticing the spectacular view. Logan's booted steps on the wood floor alerted her to his presence before he spoke.

"I'm all set with these papers."

Sharlie turned. "I can't believe you bought this place." Unshed tears blurred her vision. She couldn't control her emotions any more. Seeing the house was too much.

Logan stood, motionless, his vivid gaze locked on hers.

She gave a shaky laugh. "I can't even remember how many times we used to drive past this place. Dreaming." Those dreams were gone now. A tear broke free and rolled down her cheek.

"Please don't cry." He stepped forward, dropping the papers he held. His thumb stroked her cheek, wiping away the tear. "I never could bear to see you cry."

The words whispered across Sharlie's skin as

Logan lowered his head. She closed her eyes when the first touch of his mouth feathered across her own.

"Logan." His name came out on a sigh as he gathered her close.

Fresh moisture sprang to her eyes at the gentle pressure of his lips on hers. His earlier kisses had been passionate, sometimes brutal. His cruel words had cut deep into her heart. This time the tender touch of his kiss threatened to shatter her soul for a whole different reason.

Comfort flooded through her. She felt safe and protected in his arms. But she had no right to be there. He had been the one who'd left, but she had ruined all of their dreams.

She pushed away, needing to distance herself from him. They stared into one another's eyes. His glowed with an intense emotion she felt sure was mirrored in her own.

"I...I have to get back to work." Her voice trembled. Kneeling, she shoved the scattered papers together and clutched them protectively to her chest, carrying them like a shield.

"I have to go," she repeated, turning and heading out of the room. She was through the front door and halfway down the steps when Logan's voice reached her.

"Sharlie, wait."

But she had made it to the safety of her car. She started the car and put it in gear. Gravel spewed under the wheels as she sped away from Logan, his house, and the pain of what could never be.

****

Logan stared after the retreating car. "Damn," he cursed, then twisted his lips into a grimace of a smile. He'd been using that word a lot. Ever since he'd walked into The Corral and found Sharlie there. His tongue touched his lower lip, and he cursed again. He could still taste her.

He turned to head back into the house, but paused to survey the façade of the ranch. He hadn't expected her reaction to seeing the place. It had upset her.

She'd remembered how they'd used to drive by it back in high school. Right before they'd head out to the deserted railroad tracks and make love in his old second-hand pickup.

He wondered for the thousandth time why Sharlie had thrown it all away.

## Chapter Seven

Logan was waiting for Sharlie when she walked into The Corral. Their eyes met and held for several long moments before he spoke.

"Can we talk?"

The quiet tone and earnest expression in his eyes almost undid her. She had thought of nothing but him since leaving his ranch the day before. She knew what he wanted to talk about. He wanted to talk about what had upset her. And she wouldn't—couldn't—talk about that. Not with anyone. Especially not with Logan.

"I have a lot of work to do." She walked past him, but he grasped her arm, the look in his eyes halting her more so than his gentle grip.

"Please."

"I can't." She couldn't explain it to him. Her emotions were still running too high from his kiss. His gentle, tender, comforting kiss.

The thought brought tears to her eyes, and she willed them not to fall.

Logan framed her face in his hand, the gesture achingly familiar. "Why won't you tell me what's wrong? Why are you pushing me away? You used to tell me everything."

"That was before. Things have changed." She hated the way her voice trembled. She hated the weak feeling that made her want to lean further into him and bury herself in his embrace.

She forced herself to step back. His hand fell to his side.

She turned away.

"Don't walk away from me," he pleaded softly.

Sharlie glanced back, then gave in to the look in his eyes. She swayed toward him. His hands came to rest on her shoulders. The strength of his gentle touch made her feel delicate and fragile. He looked into her eyes, emotion flickering in his.

"Tell me that kiss didn't mean anything. Then I'll let you go." His hands tightened for a moment, as if to prevent that from happening.

She was trapped by his look, his touch, the memories both provoked. Tell him his kiss meant nothing?

She wanted to laugh out loud, although the situation was far from funny. His kiss had meant everything. It had been the Logan she knew, had longed for. She'd never tell him though, because then she'd have to tell him all of it.

"It was a mistake." She lowered her eyes to hide the lie.

Logan went still, and she risked a glance at him. His irises had darkened with anger. The sight somehow gave Sharlie strength. This was the new Logan, the one she could face.

"It sure as hell didn't feel like a mistake."

"Wha...what?"

"Something that felt so right couldn't be a mistake. You felt it too, don't deny it. When you pressed your body into mine." Logan took a step closer.

Her breath caught in her throat as his body brushed hers.

"I could feel you, Sharlie. All of you. When your mouth opened under mine," the pad of his thumb traced her lower lip, "it was so sweet. The look in your eyes. You looked at me like I was the only one in the world who could take away your pain."

She swallowed, mesmerized by his words. Slowly, she shook her head. No one could take away

79

her pain. Not even Logan. Especially not Logan.

She was so confused. Her body shivered from the slight contact with his. Her mouth trembled with the need to feel his lips against hers. Yesterday, Logan had been the source of her comfort, but she couldn't forget he'd also hurt her since he'd returned. And regardless of that, they had no future together.

She pulled away from him.

He grabbed her arm. "Don't walk away from me."

"Leave her alone."

Sharlie looked up in surprise as Zach's angry tone echoed down the hallway. He approached with a menacing look on his face.

"Zach," she began.

"Stay out of this, Rawlings," Logan snarled. "It doesn't concern you."

"Get your hands off of her. She doesn't want to talk to you."

"How do you know who she wants to talk to?"

The two men squared off, staring each other down.

Neither looked away from the other when Sharlie spoke. "Stop it right now. You're both acting like children."

She pulled her arm from Logan's grasp.

He looked down at her. "We're not through. Call off your watch dog."

Out of the corner of her eye, she saw Zach bristle at the remark, but her gaze remained focused on the raven-haired man who so dominated her thoughts these days. "We are through. We don't have anything to talk about."

She turned to Zach. "And, Zach, this doesn't have anything to do with you. Please stay out of it."

She walked away, feeling two pair of eyes boring into her back as she went. In her office she collapsed into her chair and lowered her head onto her arms on her desk. She couldn't take too much more of this. She had to get away from Logan.

****

The previous night at The Corral had been hell. Sharlie had spent the entire evening watching the stairs leading down into the bar waiting for Logan. She'd been half afraid he wouldn't come down, and half afraid he would.

He hadn't come down.

Pete had said Logan needed to finish up some things out at his place and wouldn't be working that night. Sharlie figured he had been avoiding her.

Which was fine, that's what she planned to do herself. Avoid Logan. At all costs.

Now it was a new work night, and he was due to arrive at the bar at any moment.

"Sharlie?"

She jumped. "Damnit, Zach. Don't scare me like that."

"Scare you? I said your name. What's the matter with you?"

"Nothing. Why would anything be the matter?"

Zach leaned against the bar. The Corral hadn't opened for business yet, and they had the place to themselves. "You tell me." He looked into her eyes. "You haven't been yourself lately. You looked pretty upset when you returned from running errands the other day. Where were you?"

"Nowhere."

"Running errands nowhere?" Zach's voice sounded skeptical.

"Pete asked me to take care of a few things for him, that's all."

"What kinds of things?"

"What is this, the third degree?"

Zach threw up his hands. "Whoa, easy there. You looked upset. I thought maybe I could help."

Sharlie gazed at him for a long moment. She

shouldn't be taking things out on Zach. "I'm sorry. I have a lot of things on my mind lately."

"Do those things have anything to do with Logan Reed?" For once there wasn't anger in Zach's voice as he referred to Logan. Only a quiet resignation.

She couldn't lie to him. He'd been a good friend for too long. "Yes." She looked into his understanding eyes. "Oh, Zach, I'm so confused."

"Ah, honey. Come here." He pulled her into his arms.

Sharlie went into his embrace. She found the comfort she sought, but nothing could compare to being held by Logan.

"Do you want to talk about it?"

Where would she start? And she knew deep down that Zach wasn't the best person to tell.

"Are you in love with him?"

She moved out of Zach's embrace to look at him. A shadow of pain darkened his eyes, but she had to be honest. "I loved him a long time ago."

"Do you still love him now?"

"I don't know." Her whisper was broken. Getting emotionally involved with anyone was dangerous. Falling in love with Logan again was down right insane. She wouldn't let it happen. She *couldn't* let it happen.

"Ah, hell." Zach pulled her back into his arms.

"What am I going to do?" She asked the question more of herself than of the man who held her. "I—" She broke off as Logan walked down into the bar.

He took one look at her in Zach's arms, and there was murder in his eyes. He turned on his heel.

Sharlie took a step toward him. She called after him.

But he was already halfway up the stairs. He didn't even glance back at the sound of his name.

"Damn," she murmured under her breath.

"I'm sorry."

She smiled at Zach. "Don't be. None of this is your fault."

"Maybe if I talked to him?"

Sharlie laughed without humor. "No, I don't think that would help. Logan thinks we're together."

"Together? You and me?"

"Yeah."

For a brief moment, Zach looked pleased. "Then maybe I should talk to him. Tell him the truth."

"It doesn't matter. Logan and I have too many unresolved things between us. This is a misunderstanding."

Zach looked at her. "Why haven't you told him the truth?"

Sharlie lowered her eyes. "I'm only guessing that's what he thinks. We haven't talked about it."

"Maybe you should."

"Yeah, maybe." Zach wasn't at the heart of her problems with Logan. If he thought she was with Zach, maybe that was for the best.

She shook off the disturbing thoughts. "Well, I guess we need to be getting to work. This place'll be jammed soon."

"If you need anything..."

"Thanks." Would things be simpler if she could fall in love with Zach? Sharlie didn't know. She couldn't offer him everything he deserved. Besides, even he wouldn't want her if he knew the truth.

****

They were busier than they'd been since the rodeo had left town. Cooler weather had set in at night, and many people were looking for indoor activities to pursue. Sharlie welcomed the crowd. It kept her mind off Logan. She'd managed to avoid talking with him all evening, a feat she viewed with mixed emotions.

For his part, Logan made no attempt at conversation either, but tossed angry glares across the bar at her whenever their eyes met. After one of these unnerving stares, Sharlie turned and almost collided with Jake.

"Where's the fire?" she joked, noticing the bucket he held in one hand.

"No fire." Jake laughed, indicating the mop he held in the other. "A spill at the main bar."

"Thanks for taking care of that." She'd been so caught up in thoughts of Logan she hadn't even noticed. Damn the man.

"Just doin' my job, ma'am." Jake grinned and headed off to the bar.

A customer brushed past him. He lost his footing on the wet floor and slipped. The bucket flew from his hands, hitting a stack of glasses resting on a nearby table. Sharlie watched in horror as they toppled to the floor, crashing and shattering around him.

She hurried to him and knelt beside him, heedless of the broken glass and the wet seeping into her jeans. His arm was cut and bleeding in several places, the blood mixing with the mess on the floor.

A crowd had gathered by this time, and Sharlie heard Zach's command. "Alright, everybody. Stand back."

The curious onlookers obeyed the authority in his voice, parting to allow him to approach from one side. Out of the corner of her eye, Sharlie saw Logan heading toward her from the other direction.

"Jake? Are you okay?" She brushed the hair off his forehead. Her hand come away smeared with blood.

She stared at it. From what seemed like a long distance away, she heard someone calling her name. The blood-stained hand wavered in front of her eyes. Blackness washed over her. She swayed.

And was caught up in strong arms.

Logan's familiar intoxicating scent filled her

senses, clearing her head. She clutched at him, smearing the blood on his white shirt. "The blood," she whispered.

"Sharlie? Are you hurt?" Fear lurked in Logan's voice and eyes as he ran his hands over her.

"It's not her blood," Zach broke in, joining the group kneeling on the floor beside Jake.

"Sharlie?" Logan cradled her face in his hands, forcing her to look at him. Concern had replaced the earlier anger in his eyes.

"I...I'm okay. I hate the sight of blood." She laughed, but it was shaky. "I would make a terrible nurse."

Logan pulled her close again, his steady heartbeat comforting beneath her cheek. She squeezed her eyes closed, pressing her face deeper into his broad chest, trying to shut out the images flooding her mind.

"You all right?" he asked Jake.

"I'm fine," Jake replied, sitting up. "Some of the glass hit me when it shattered. It's only a few scratches."

"Not this time, buddy," Zach interjected, pushing him back down. "I think you're going to need a few stitches. These are pretty deep. We need to get you to the hospital."

Sharlie shivered. Hospitals brought back too many bad memories.

Logan stroked her hair, murmuring in her ear. "Come on, honey. Let's get you out of here." He rose to his feet, pulling her with him. "You okay here, Zach?"

"Yeah, I've got it. Thanks." Zach nodded toward Sharlie. "Get her out of here."

The last thing she heard as Logan led her away was Zach instructing one of the bartenders to call an ambulance.

She wasn't quite sure how they got there, but

the next thing she knew Logan had her seated in Pete's office and was pressing a glass into her hands.

"Drink this."

"No, I...I'm okay."

"Drink it." Logan raised the glass to her lips, giving her no choice in the matter.

Sharlie obeyed. Her eyes watered as the strong liquid burned down her throat. She looked at him over the rim of the glass. His eyes reflected his worry.

She laid her hand against the side of his face, feeling the slight abrasion of whiskers. "Thank you."

Before Logan could reply, the door opened and Pete dashed in. "What happened? Honey, are you all right?" He knelt on the floor in front of her chair, concern etched into his features. His eyes whisked over her.

"It's not her blood," Logan said. "Jake slipped and fell. Some glasses shattered around him. He'll be okay, but he needs a few stitches."

Pete nodded, his gaze still riveted on Sharlie.

"I'm okay, Pete. Really. There was a lot of blood." Blood always made her queasy. It also reminded her of that night long ago. When everything had changed.

"Take her home."

She looked up at Pete's words. "What? No. I'm fine. I thought Jake was really hurt."

Logan squatted, joining Pete in front of her chair. She could tell from the look in his eyes that he didn't believe her.

"Pete's right, sweetheart. You need to get out of here."

"I'm working," Sharlie protested, looking from one determined set of eyes to another.

Pete snorted. "I ain't retired yet, little lady. I can handle things around here.

"But, Jake..."

86

"Is going to be fine. Kate volunteered to ride to the hospital with him. Zach will be downstairs to handle things."

"See?" Logan said. He rose and pulled her up. "Everything is taken care of here. Let's get you taken care of."

She waved a hand dismissively. "I'm fine." She noticed her hand was spotted with dry blood and winced.

"Humor me," Logan said. "Do you need to get your purse or anything?"

Sharlie gave in. "It's in my office."

"I'll get it," Pete volunteered.

In no time, he'd returned with the bag.

"Thanks." She smiled at him.

"You're welcome." He kissed her cheek, then turned to Logan. "You take good care of her, you hear?"

Logan smiled. "I hear."

Pete nodded.

Sharlie allowed Logan to lead her out of the bar and settle her in the passenger seat of his pickup. It felt so good to be taken care of. Most of the time she was the one in charge. She relaxed against the back of the seat and closed her eyes. She didn't realize she'd dozed off until the soft touch of a hand on her cheek woke her.

Opening her eyes, her gaze collided with Logan's.

"We're home, sweetheart."

Why did he keep calling her that? She'd tell him to stop later. For now it sounded too good.

They walked into her apartment, and Logan flipped on the light with the switch by the door. He guided her through the living room to the bedroom beyond. He turned on a lamp on the nightstand beside the bed, flooding the room with soft light, then flipped back the covers with one smooth motion. "Lie down."

Somewhere deep inside, Sharlie knew she should protest. She hadn't been the one injured tonight. But it felt so good to have Logan looking after her. She would fantasize for a little longer that he still cared about her. She sank down on the bed.

Logan smiled as she acquiesced, then disappeared through the door. She heard cabinets opening and water running in the bathroom, and then he reappeared with a wet washcloth.

The bed dipped beneath his weight as he sat down beside her. He used the cloth to wipe her hands free of all traces of blood.

"Do you want to get out of these clothes?"

Sharlie blinked. Was Logan really sitting on her bed asking her if she wanted to take off her clothes? She glanced down at her shirt and jeans. She wore her boots, too.

A nervous giggle escaped. "I guess that would be a good idea."

"Do you still keep your pajamas under your pillow?" Logan's husky voice washed over her like a caress. His eyes held hers for a long moment, then he leaned over, his body brushing hers as he ran a hand under the pillow.

Her breath hitched.

He grinned when he pulled his hand free, triumph in his eyes, clutching a soft cotton garment. "I guess so."

"How in the world did you remember that?" she asked when he had straightened and she was able to draw a normal breath again.

"I remember a lot of things."

Logan's soft words, coupled with the intense heat in his emerald eyes zeroed in on Sharlie's heart. Their gazes locked, and she was sure he could see her heart about to beat out of her chest.

"Mickey Mouse?" he guessed as he shook out the

shirt in his hand.

"Of course," she replied as casually as she could.

She clutched his arm when he rose from the bed. "Are you leaving?" She heard, and hated, the panic lacing her voice.

"While you change. Let me know when you're set." He turned at the door. "Do you need anything else?"

Sharlie shook her head, then as soon as he left, hurried to divest herself of her clothes and slip into the comfortable T-shirt. She crawled beneath the cozy covers of her bed and waited for Logan to return. In the morning she would despise the weakness that made her need Logan to be there, but for now she would enjoy the moment. Regrets would come later. She knew that only too well.

A knock on the door preceded Logan's voice through the thin wood. "Are you decent?"

"Yeah, come on in."

He entered the bedroom, pausing when he saw her propped up against the pillows. His gaze found hers, then skipped to the pile of discarded clothes on the floor. He swallowed.

He cleared his throat. "I thought you might like some tea." The rattle of the spoon against the ceramic betrayed the slight trembling of his hand as he handed her the cup.

"Thanks."

"You're welcome." Logan paced the small room, as if not sure what to do with himself.

"Come sit with me."

His eyes snapped to hers. "I don't think—" he began.

"Please?" Sharlie knew she wasn't playing fair, but she was tired of hiding her feelings. She needed comfort from him. He hadn't been there twelve years ago when she'd needed him, but he was there now. He couldn't change the past, but for now he could help hold the memories at bay.

He sat on the side of the bed. "Is your tea okay?"

"It's perfect." Her gaze searched his face, then drifted lower to his wide shoulders. A smear of blood marred his white shirt. She turned away.

"What?" Logan asked with concern.

"You have blood on your shirt." She had been so engrossed in Logan's presence she hadn't noticed until now.

He glanced down and cursed. "Damn. I'm sorry. I didn't realize." He stood and unbuttoned the stained garment, pulling it from his jeans as he did so.

Sharlie's mouth went dry. As each button came undone, the shirt parted further, revealing the dark mat of hair on his muscled torso. The white fabric contrasted with the deep tan of his skin. The final button came free, and Logan shrugged the shirt off his shoulders. He tossed it to the floor where it came to rest on top of her jeans.

He froze. And raised his eyes to her.

His eyes had darkened. She noted this briefly, before her gaze was drawn back to his magnificent chest. As a teenager, Logan's body had been well developed, but as a man he was the sexiest she'd ever seen. Crisp curling hair, thicker now than in his younger years, covered his chest, but couldn't hide the muscles there.

Sharlie swallowed, her gaze following the hair as it tapered near his navel and disappeared into the waistband of his jeans.

"Don't look at me like that," Logan warned, his voice deeper than before

Her eyes met his.

"Don't look at me like that either," he growled.

She must have made some inarticulate sound in her throat, a feat she thought impossible in her speechless state, because with a muttered curse,

Logan crossed to the bed and dropped to his knees beside it. His trembling hand cupped her face, then smoothed the hair back from her forehead. "I can't stop thinking about you."

Sharlie felt rather than heard the words as Logan's mouth consumed hers. She moaned deep in her throat. His answering groan vibrated against her lips. His tongue demanded entrance. She opened for him. He caressed the sensitive flesh inside her lower lip, then delved deeper to mate with hers.

The contact caused a kick deep in the pit of her stomach. She shuddered.

He levered himself from the floor onto the bed. His weight crushed her into the pillows. The muscles she had earlier devoured with her eyes felt hot and hard beneath her hands as she splayed them across his wide back. She caressed each bicep. Her hands slid from his shoulders to the barrier of his jeans. She couldn't get enough of him.

This was Logan. So different in a man's body, yet so familiar, she ached.

Their harsh breathing reverberated in the small room, closing in on them as Logan dragged his lips from hers to trail moist kisses down her neck. His open mouth slid to the edge of her T-shirt, raising goosebumps in its wake. He gently bit the lobe of her ear, then hurried his lips back to hers when she sighed and shivered.

His mouth ravaged hers until she moved restlessly beneath him. His hand slid under the hem of her shirt, gliding up her damp skin until it closed over one breast. The peak hardened in response.

An answering tug began deep in the core of her womanhood. She thrust against his hand, wanting more of his touch.

Her eyes flew open when he pulled away from her and sat up. He dragged a hand through his thick, dark hair. A journey her hands had taken moments before. She watched as he struggled for control, finally releasing a deep breath and meeting her eyes.

"We can't do this."

Sharlie couldn't believe her ears. "Why not? Don't you want me?" Tears sprang to her eyes, and she dashed them away, not willing to allow them to fall.

"Not want you?" Logan laughed without humor, the sound harsh and biting. He shifted, straddling her, then grasped her hips in his hands. He hauled her up into the cradle of his thighs.

She cried out, feeling the hard steel of him pressing against her softest part. Her thin nightgown and panties were no match for the heat burning through the denim of his jeans.

"Does that answer your question?" His voice was rough with need.

The feel of him pressed against her made speaking difficult. She remembered what it felt like to have him inside her. "Then why?"

"Not like this. Not when you're too emotional about what happened tonight to think clearly."

Sharlie wanted to protest, but deep down knew he was right. He had more sense than she did. She couldn't get involved with him again. Her desire faded as quickly as it had come.

"I won't pretend to guess why you were so upset tonight. I know it was more than Jake's accident. You needed comfort from anyone who would give it."

"That's not true," Sharlie whispered.

Logan smiled. "Well, maybe not anyone. But when we make love," his eyes darkened with promise, "I want it to be because you want to make love. Not for any other reason."

For a brief instant, hope bloomed deep inside her, in a heart that had been shattered long ago. Then reality set in. A second chance was impossible.

Even if they put the past behind them and forgave one another for the hurts they'd each caused, there was still so much he didn't know.

He wouldn't want her if he knew. But for tonight, she needed him. For one night, she'd be selfish, then she'd let him go so he could have the life he deserved. The life she couldn't give him. "Will you at least hold me?"

He paused. "Yeah, I can do that." He arranged the tangled covers around them both, tucking her against his side, and reached over to click off the light.

She rested her head in the curve of his shoulder. The hair on his chest tickled her cheek. The steady beat of his heart pulsed beneath her ear. She breathed in the scent of spicy aftershave and man that was Logan. She felt the light brush of his lips against her hair and sighed in contentment. She remembered the times they'd lain in Logan's small bed. Being here with him now was so familiar, yet so different.

His whisper reached through the first vestiges of sleep. "Goodnight, sweetheart."

****

Soon Sharlie's even breathing told Logan she'd fallen asleep. He shifted, trying to find a position to ease his discomfort. He reached under the covers and released the button on his jeans, knowing it would do little to assuage the pressure there.

Sharlie stirred in her sleep, snuggling closer to him. The softness of her breast pressed into his ribs, and he bit back a groan.

She had needed him tonight. The thought pleased him. She had turned to him for comfort, not Zach. Had he been wrong about the two of them? Anger had burned in him when he'd walked down the stairs into The Corral earlier and saw her in the other man's arms. After he'd spent the day thinking

93

about how good it had felt to hold her in *his* arms again. And so right.

Why had she sent him away years ago? It sure seemed like she wanted him back in her life, especially after tonight. After all these years, maybe they were finally going to have the chance to be together.

Her distress over Jake tonight troubled him. True, Jake had been hurt, but relatively speaking, his injuries were minor. Something else had upset her. Logan intended to find out what it was.

Chapter Eight

Sharlie woke the next morning feeling utterly relaxed. She stretched and encountered the empty expanse of sheet next to her.

She stopped mid-stretch. Had she dreamt Logan spent the night with her? Turning, she noticed the other pillow still bore the impression of his head. She buried her face in the pillow and inhaled the spicy scent clinging to it.

Sounds filled the usually still apartment. Plates and glasses clinked. The refrigerator door opened and closed. Logan's cheery, but off-key, whistle reminded her he'd never been able to carry a tune.

The smell of frying bacon prompted her to swing her legs over the side of the bed. Her pulse quickened. What would she say to Logan? What would he say to her? Would he expect something?

She needed to put an end to whatever it was they'd started last night. It wouldn't be fair to lead him on. With her heart beating wildly in her chest, she padded barefoot through the living room and into the kitchen.

Logan stood at the stove, a spatula in hand. He wore nothing but his jeans. His bare feet looked out of place where they rested on her daisy rug. The jeans were zipped, but unbuttoned, giving Sharlie an intimate view of the hair that whorled around his navel.

Unable to stop herself, her eyes roved over his bare chest, admiring the play of muscles there. His hair was damp from the shower and curled in an enticing manner over his forehead. She had the urge to run her fingers through the wet strands and brush them away from his face.

"Good morning," she said, drawing his attention to her.

He looked over. "Mornin'."

She'd almost forgotten how his eyes crinkled at the corners when he smiled. But she did recognize the look in his eyes as his gaze slipped down her body, from the top of her sleep-tousled head, past the Mickey Mouse T-shirt, down her legs, all the way to her bare toes.

He drew his eyes back up to hers. "I don't think I've ever seen you right after you've woken up in the morning."

They'd never been able to wake up together. In high school they'd made love in his truck or his bedroom, but she always needed to be home before morning.

"There's not much to see," Sharlie answered. She hadn't even brushed her hair or teeth.

"I'll be the judge of that," Logan said. He turned back to the stove. "I hope you like eggs and bacon."

"Sounds great." She scooted closer to peer over his shoulder, but resisted the urge to touch him. "Is there anything I can do?"

"Pour us some orange juice." He tossed a quick glance behind him. "I hope you don't mind, I made myself at home."

"Not at all." She busied herself with the juice, then stepped out of his way so he could dish up their breakfast. The kitchen was so small, she stepped right into him. Up against his bare chest. Her breath caught.

Their eyes met and held. Suddenly the scrambled eggs weren't the only thing heating up the kitchen.

"Uh, sorry—"

"Ooops, I—"

They spoke at the same time, then laughed together, easing the tension that crackled in the air.

They ate in silence for a while, forks scraping across plates the only sound in the room. She had never realized how intimate eating breakfast with a man could be. Especially when the man in question was as sexy as Logan. She remembered his bare chest crushed against her last night. Her body grew warm and tingled at the memory. How would she be feeling if they had made love? She couldn't imagine being any more aware of him.

Finished with her bacon and eggs, Sharlie had nothing more to do but stare at him over the rim of her juice glass. She shifted in her chair and recrossed her legs under the table. No one had the right to look that good.

Logan finished and tossed down his napkin. He glanced up and caught her staring at him. His face wore a solemn expression. She got the feeling he was trying to read deep into her thoughts.

She had things she didn't want him to see in her eyes, so she looked down at her empty plate. "This was great. Thanks."

"You're welcome."

"Thank you for last night. I don't know what got into me. I usually don't fall apart like that."

"It's tough to see someone you care about hurting."

Something in the tone of his voice told her he wasn't referring to her reaction to Jake's accident. She raised her eyes to his, then stared at him for endless seconds before clearing her throat. "I wonder how—"

"Jake's fine. I already talked to Pete this morning."

She nodded, pleased at his thoughtfulness in checking on Jake.

"Do you think Zach will be upset he didn't take

you home last night?"

She knew Logan's casual tone hid a rainbow of emotions. "Look, there's something you need to know. Zach and I aren't together." She couldn't use Zach against Logan any longer. Although it would give her the perfect out, it wasn't fair to her friend.

"I know."

That wasn't the reaction she'd anticipated. "You know?"

Logan nodded. "You wouldn't have kissed me like that last night if you were involved with someone else. You never would have let me spend the night in your bed."

"But we didn't—" Heat suffused her face. She wasn't used to talking so openly about sex.

"That doesn't matter. I know you, Sharlie. You wouldn't have even let me hold you if there were someone else." His heated gaze held hers for long moments.

What would he say if she told him no one had been in her bed since he'd left? Would he believe her? Twelve years was a long time, but after Logan, she hadn't allowed herself to get that close to someone again.

He broke the intense stare and rose. He cleared the dishes and stacked them in the sink.

"Leave them. I'll do them later. You've done enough."

Logan grinned. "If you insist. Dishes were never my favorite. By the way, what are you going to do today? Besides the dishes, that is."

Sharlie shrugged. "Not much. I'm off tonight."

"How'd you like to come shopping with me?"

"Shopping? For what?"

Logan's light demeanor became serious. "Yesterday Pete and I signed the final papers on The Corral. His last day is Friday."

"You bought The Corral?"

Logan nodded. In one step he crossed the tiny kitchen and hunkered down in front of her chair. "I need to know how you feel about that."

How did she feel about it? She wasn't sure. She thought of all the reasons she hadn't wanted him to buy the bar. Why she hadn't wanted him around at all.

He didn't know about the baby. That wasn't the reason he'd returned after all these years. If he didn't know now, there was no reason for him to ever find out.

She'd have to make sure that what had almost happened last night didn't happen again. From now on, things would be strictly business between them. Maybe someday they could even be friends. She gazed into Logan's eyes, knowing her answer was important to him. "I think Pete's leaving it in good hands."

Logan still didn't look convinced. "Are you sure?"

"Yes."

Logan closed his eyes and exhaled with a soft rushing sound. He opened them and smiled at her. "I'm glad."

"Me too. Now what's all this got to do with shopping?"

"Trust a woman to remember the shopping part of the question," Logan teased, then grunted when she swatted him on the arm. "Pete's going away party is Friday night. I figured you could help me get that together. Seemed kind of like a woman thing." He rose from the balls of his feet before she could sock him again.

It seemed like ages ago that they'd argued about the party. A lot had changed in that short time. She rose from her chair and tried to look as threatening as possible in bare feet and a Mickey Mouse T-shirt. She gave him her most intimidating look. "I'll do it. But only because it's for Pete."

"Great. I'll take what I can get. How soon can you be ready?"

"Give me half an hour."

"Sounds good. I need to run out to my truck and grab a spare shirt."

"There's an extra key in the bowl on the table by the door. Then you won't have to be buzzed in."

Sharlie waited until Logan had left the apartment before she scurried into the bathroom for a quick shower. His damp towel hung from the hook on the back of the door. She touched it, jealous of the soft cloth that had skimmed over Logan's naked body, absorbing the moisture from his shower.

She stepped under the spray of the shower. The cap of the shampoo bottle was open. Another teasing reminder of Logan's presence. What it would be like to share the small stall with him?

As she lathered her body, her hand brushed over her breasts. Her nipples tightened at the memory of Logan's hand cupping her. So much for keeping things all business. Maybe spending the day with him wasn't such a hot idea.

She rinsed, then stepped out onto the bath mat to dry herself. Since she hadn't brought a change of clothes into the bathroom with her, she'd have to put her T-shirt back on or walk out in a towel. She bit her lip, then wrapped the small scrap of terrycloth securely around her, making a mental note to invest in some bigger bath towels.

She opened the door a crack and peered out. "Logan?"

No response. Sharlie hastened across the hall into her bedroom. She put on jeans and a denim shirt. Not bothering with a hair dryer, she pulled her hair away from her face and twisted an elastic band around her ponytail. When Logan returned she was in the bathroom applying a light layer of make-up.

"I'm almost ready," she called.

He appeared in the doorway and leaned negligently against the jam. A quick glance told her he sported a white pocketed T-shirt, and he'd put his boots back on. Too bad. But most stores had that 'no shoes no shirt' rule anyway.

Feeling his gaze upon her as she used a curved brush to apply mascara to her lashes, Sharlie experienced the same sensation she'd had at the breakfast table. Putting on makeup had never been an intimate experience before, but somehow, with Logan watching her go through motions she'd performed hundreds of times, it was.

She made quick work of brushing her teeth—nothing intimate about spitting into the sink—and turned to face him. "I'm set."

"Let's hit the road."

He outlined his plan as they headed into town.

"It sounds great. Pete will be so surprised." Some of Sharlie's animation faded. "I'm going to miss him."

Logan reached over and placed a hand on her knee. The gesture was meant to comfort, but her flesh warmed and her heart beat an erratic rhythm.

"Everyone will, but I'm sure we're not going to be rid of him that easily. He's put a lot of himself into that bar. He won't be able to stay away."

"You won't mind if he comes around now that you're the owner?"

"Of course not. I've become sort of fond of the old coot since I've been here. He kind of grows on you."

Sharlie laughed at his description of Pete. It warmed her heart to know Logan had come to care for the man she loved like a father.

While they shopped, Logan related stories from the years he'd spent developing his rodeo camp. The antics of the kids he spoke of made Sharlie want to cry as much as she laughed. He truly loved children.

Kids of his own would surely play an important

role in Logan's future. The thought caused a stab of pain in her heart and strengthened her resolve not to get more involved with him.

They shopped for hours, buying everything from streamers and balloons to a sheet cake decorated with tiny boots and cowboy hats. At each store Logan pulled out a credit card or paid for the purchases they'd made with cash. He didn't even blink an eye as the bills added up and steadily grew.

At last they found time to grab a bite to eat at Bubba's Diner.

As Logan reached for the bill, she stopped him. "I can pay my own way."

Logan waved her comment away. "Don't worry about it. It's my treat."

"You can't buy me, Logan."

He stopped cold, his eyes boring into her. "What the hell is that supposed to mean?"

"All day long you've been throwing money away like it grows on trees."

"So?"

"So stop trying to show off your money to me."

"Is that what you think I'm doing? Rubbing my money in your face?"

She lowered her gaze from his, then raised it again. "That's what it seems like sometimes."

Logan sighed. "This is crazy."

In an instant Sharlie was defensive. "What's so crazy about it?"

"Don't you see? It's like *deja vu*?"

"What?"

"We've talked about this before. We used to have this conversation every time we went out and you paid for something."

Comprehension dawned on her. Logan was right. In high school she'd been the one with money, and he'd been the one to protest her paying for things.

102

"Do you remember what you used to say to me?"

Sharlie nodded. She'd always asked if her money changed the way he felt about her.

"And do you remember what I used to say to you?"

"You said money didn't change the way you felt about me. You still lov—" She couldn't bring herself to talk of the love they'd once shared.

"Right. So do you see me in a different way since I have money now?"

She considered for a moment. The fact that he had money didn't bother her. She'd never been one to judge a person's worth by how big their checkbook was. But knowing he had gotten some of it from her father *did* bother her.

She looked into his eyes and decided she needed to be honest. About this. Some things were best left unsaid.

"It doesn't bother me that you have money now. It bothers me how you got some of it."

"You mean that check from your father."

She was taken aback by his blunt statement. She hadn't expected him to talk about it so directly. "Yes."

Logan looked at her, seeming to weigh what he was going to say. "Can we forget about that check? Pretend like it didn't exist."

Her first thought was that it was an easy thing for him to do. It had gotten him started on the right track, and now he had all of the things in life that he had wanted. Then she changed her mind. Maybe it was time to put the past, at least that part of it, behind them.

"I guess we can do that."

"I think there's something you should know about that check."

"What?"

"I —"

"Are you all set here, luv?" The heavyset waitress interrupted, taking the money Logan had laid on the table.

Logan looked at Sharlie. "Yeah, we're all set here." He gave the waitress a disarming smile, and she blushed like a teenager. "Keep the change."

"Thanks, luv. You two kids have a nice day. Try to stay dry out there. Looks like a storm's comin' pretty fast." With a wink at Logan she waddled away.

Sharlie suppressed a grin. "You certainly have a way with women."

Logan rose from the booth and grabbed her hand to pull her out, too. "The only woman I want to have my way with is you." He kissed her.

She caught her breath at the passion that flared deep inside her in response to his words. The brief touch of his lips on hers had her craving more. Much more. Which was bad.

Their gazes met and held.

"We'd better go," she said to break the intense silence. She was getting in too deep with Logan. She couldn't start a relationship with him again. It wouldn't be fair to him. The sooner she told him the only thing that could ever be between them was friendship, the better.

When they got back to his house, she would tell him.

Outside the day had darkened and ominous clouds roiled across the leaden sky. Gusts of wind swirled around them, and Sharlie shivered as they tore through her hair and clothes.

Logan glanced up and frowned. "That storm's getting close."

As if in agreement, lightning flashed and thunder rolled in the distance. Huge drops of rain began to fall, splattering on the ground.

"Let's go." He grabbed her hand and ran toward

the truck.

They sprang into the cab, laughing, as the rain started in earnest. The drops beat a staccato rhythm on the roof. The temperature outside had dropped, but inside the truck the enclosed space was cozy and warm.

A few minutes later they pulled into the curving gravel drive in front of his ranch, the storm on their heels. They made it into the sanctuary of the house and closed the door behind them as the storm hit in all its fury.

"Phew, that was close," Sharlie panted, then exclaimed in surprise as Logan flicked the lights on. "Wow. This place sure looks different."

The room was filled with furniture. A sofa and love seat were arranged around the fireplace. An oversized chair stood off to one side. An entertainment center held a large screen TV and various electronic equipment. Two additional recliners faced the large picture window, which now revealed only the darkness outside, broken by an occasional flash of lightning. A low table containing assorted magazines and books stood between the chairs. Soft light spilled into the room from tracks set in the high ceiling. Everything was done in neutral shades that brought to mind images of the outdoors.

"I love what you've done with the place."

Logan laughed. "Quite an improvement, hey? I felt like I was living in a cave. The furniture was delivered yesterday. Make yourself at home. I'll light a fire." He squatted in front of the fireplace and stacked logs inside the grate.

Sharlie sat on the couch, kicked off her shoe boots, and curled her feet beneath her. She enjoyed the rain's steady tattoo against the windows and roof. The rolling thunder echoed around them as the center of the storm drew nearer.

Soon the crackle of the fire whispered through the room. Logan rose. "Can I get you anything? Tea or something?"

"No, I'm fine," Sharlie said, then jumped when a loud crash of thunder rattled the windows. The lights flickered. She laughed nervously, but whether from the storm or from worrying about what she was going to tell Logan, she wasn't sure. "The storm's picking up."

"I haven't seen one like this in quite a while." Logan moved to the large picture window to gaze out at the foreboding sky.

Another brilliant flash of lightning lit the landscape outside, throwing his form into dark relief against the brightness for brief seconds. He looked strong and sure outlined against nature's display. She had the urge to go to him and wrap her arms around his waist. Instead, she wrapped her hands around her arms and hugged herself.

Logan turned from the window. "Are you cold?"

"No." She paused. "Can I talk to you about something?"

Before Logan could reply, another flash of lightning was followed in an instant by a mighty crash of thunder. This time the lights flickered and went out. The soft glow from the fire lit the room.

"I was afraid of that," Logan muttered.

"Do you have any candles?" Sharlie rose from the sofa.

"Yeah, I think so. Trouble is I'm not sure where. Most of my stuff is still in boxes."

"How about a flashlight?"

"I definitely have one of those in the kitchen." Logan disappeared through the nearby doorway.

Sharlie stayed put. She didn't want to stub a toe moving around in the darkened, unfamiliar surroundings. The fireplace's dim light cast eerie shadows on the walls. The rain beat against the roof.

It sounded louder in the darkness.

Logan returned, flashlight in hand. "Well, I found it, but the batteries are nearly dead."

She laughed. "Something tells me you were never a Boy Scout."

"Give me a break," Logan defended himself. "I just moved in."

"Well, hopefully it'll last long enough for us to find some of those candles." Sharlie moved carefully to his side. "Any ideas?"

"I think there might be some in a box in my room. I haven't unpacked everything yet." He led the way down the hallway, beaming the flashlight ahead of them.

Sharlie could make out the shadowy shapes of Logan's bed and dresser when they walked into the unlit room. Last night he had overwhelmed her small bedroom with his masculine presence. In his room she felt swallowed up by the darkness.

"Everything's all jumbled from the move," Logan said, his voice coming from the shadows in one corner of the spacious room. "This might take a while."

"Can I help?" She walked toward the direction of his voice, but stumbled over a box in her path. Pain shot through her little toe. "Ouch!"

"Are you okay?" Logan's voice was nearer now.

"I'm fine. I stubbed my dang toe."

Another streak of lightning illuminated the darkened room for a moment. In those brief seconds she caught a glimpse of something that had fallen out of the box she'd tripped over.

The dim light filtering in from the rain-splattered windows didn't allow much visibility, but she made out a familiar shaped piece of paper lying on top of the other contents from the box. Her fingers trembled as she picked it up, her throat dry. A flash of lightning confirmed what the sick feeling in the pit of her stomach had already told her.

She held a check made out to Logan Reed for twenty-five thousand dollars, signed by her father.

## Chapter Nine

Thunder rumbled, farther in the distance now, as Sharlie clenched the small paper in her hand.

"Are you hurt?" Logan knelt at her side. "Sharlie?" The note of concern in his voice sharpened when she failed to respond.

Unable to speak past the lump lodged in her throat, she raised her eyes from the check to his face, visible in the waning glow of the flashlight he held. Less than an hour ago she had vowed to put the check behind her. Had said it didn't matter. But now that she held it in her hand, she wasn't so sure she'd be able to do that.

His eyes dropped to the check she clutched in her hand. She heard his quick intake of breath.

She swallowed. "Why...why do you still have this?"

"I kept it as a reminder." Logan's voice had a hard edge to it.

"A reminder?"

"Yes." He didn't elaborate.

Idly, her trembling fingers turned the check over. The endorsement line was blank. Her eyes searched out his. "If you wanted this money so badly, why didn't you cash the check?" Her voice mirrored the confusion that knotted her insides.

"If I wanted—" Logan bit off his words. He grabbed her shoulders, looking deeply into her eyes. "What do you mean?"

"Why did you ask my father for this if you weren't going to use it?"

He cursed. "I think we need to talk."

"Okay."

"I found some candles. Let's go in the family room."

Sharlie followed Logan from the room. The sick feeling in her stomach felt like a lead weight.

She sat stiffly on the edge of the couch while Logan lit the candles. The rain had nearly stopped. The crackle of the fire and the flare of a match were the only sounds in the room. That and the wild beating of her heart.

Finished, Logan joined her in the area near the fireplace. He sat down in the easy chair. His forearms rested on his knees. He studied her with an intense look, but was silent.

Sharlie squirmed under his close scrutiny and twisted a strand of hair around her finger. He had wanted to talk. Why didn't he say anything?

"Tell me what you know about that check."

She jumped when he finally spoke, breaking the oppressive silence. Her glance followed his down to the check she clutched in her damp hands. "I don't see what—"

"Please."

She couldn't figure out what game he was playing, but decided to go along. "It's why you left."

Logan nodded.

"You...you asked my father for it."

Logan's eyes narrowed, but he released a heartfelt sigh. "That's what I was afraid you were going to say."

Sharlie shook her head. "I don't understand what's going on. What are you talking about?"

Logan rose and came to squat in front of her. He looked into her eyes. "I never asked your father for that check, Sharlie."

Her heart stopped. "What?" Her voice came out in a choked whisper.

"I didn't ask your father for that check."

"But he told me..." The truth hit her like a sledgehammer. Her father had lied.

Why hadn't she seen it? She'd been so angry with Logan, so hurt by what she believed he'd done, that she hadn't been thinking straight. And she'd had the baby to think about. Still, she should have known it was Logan who could be trusted. Her gaze met his. A tear of hopelessness and sorrow rolled down her cheek.

"Why didn't you tell me? Why did you leave?" Twelve years of hurt echoed in her voice.

Logan stared into her eyes. "He said you wanted me out of your life. He told me you asked him to give me the check."

"No," Sharlie whispered brokenly. "I can't believe my father could be that cruel." But then she remembered what he'd said to her when she'd told him she was pregnant. His spiteful words had sent her out of his life forever. "And you believed him, too."

Logan nodded, a miserable look of guilt on his face.

"I don't know what to say. All those years I thought you... But what about all your money? If you didn't use the check from my father, how did you get it all?"

"I earned that money. Worked my ass off for it. I don't take handouts."

"You must have hated me."

Logan's sigh was ragged as he stroked her cheek with gentle fingers. "Don't torture yourself. None of this is our fault. Your father manipulated both of us." His thumb wiped away the tear that spilled over her lashes.

"But all those years." All the pain. All the sorrow. Everything was her father's fault. If it weren't for him, she and Logan would have had the chance to be a family. An icy fist grabbed her heart and fingers of pain spread through her chest.

She crumbled the check, then threw it in the fireplace. They silently watched it burn.

If there had ever been any doubt in Sharlie's mind that she could someday forgive her father for his cruelty, all those doubts were erased. She'd never forgive him. He had cost her so much precious time with Logan, and he had cost them a child. Tears ran unchecked down her face.

"Please don't cry, sweetheart. We're together now."

His words tore at her soul. They could never be together. "Logan, I—"

"Shhh." He placed a finger on her lips, then pulled her gently from the couch so she knelt on the floor facing him. "It's over now. We both know the truth."

The truth? They hadn't even scratched the surface, but Sharlie couldn't think with Logan touching her.

"God, I've missed you." He pulled her hair free from its confinement and ran his fingers through the strands. Her pulse quickened as he feathered open-mouthed kisses around her lips and down her throat. Although his breath was warm against her skin, she shivered from the contact, arching her neck and turning into him, her mouth searching for his, even as she told herself she needed to stop him before they went any further.

He dipped his head lower, pushing her shirt to the side to trace the delicate outline of her collarbone with his tongue.

She shuddered. His tongue slid upward to tease the corners of her mouth, still denying her the pleasure of his lips on hers.

"Please kiss me," she begged.

His gaze burned into the depths of hers. Without breaking eye contact, his lips touched hers, then darted away, only to nibble again lightly as if savoring a sweet dessert.

Sharlie moaned and closed her eyes when his mouth finally consumed hers. Gently at first, but then the moist pressure enticed her to open to him. Sweetly, passionately, tenderly, he kissed her again and again, until she clung to his shoulders.

He broke the mind-melting kiss. "Look at me."

Her eyes opened, unfocused at first. She gazed at him. His eyes reflected the candlelight surrounding them. Her breath was ragged, and her heart pounded a heavy rhythm in her chest.

"I'm going to make love to you."

Her heartbeat quickened at the bold words, and her breath caught in her throat.

"Like I should have been making love to you every night for the past twelve years if it hadn't been for that damn check." Logan pulled her close, his arms crushing her to his chest, his mouth raining kisses on the top of her head. "If only I had asked you about it. If only..."

Sharlie pulled away, placing a finger to his lips. "Don't. You can't live your life on *if only's*." God knows she had tried it often enough. "You have to live for now. You can't change the past." She closed her eyes, remembering all the times she had wished she could go back and do one thing differently. The one thing that would have changed everything.

A log in the fireplace popped and hissed. She opened her eyes. Logan was her past, but for this moment, he was her now. Did she dare, with all that was unsaid? He had to know this moment was all there could ever be between them. "Logan? I—"

Logan's mouth cut her off as it settled on hers. And then there was no room for any more words.

The weight of his body bore her backwards until she lay on the soft carpet in front of the fire. The warmth of the fireplace couldn't compete with the heat of his gaze as he unbuttoned her shirt and drew it away from her body. He unhooked the front closure of her lacy bra.

"So beautiful," he whispered huskily. He pulled his T-shirt over his head and cast it aside. The firelight played on the sculpted muscles of his chest.

She remembered their first passionate, but clumsy, attempts at making love. They had fumbled with each others' clothes, being unfamiliar with the act. Logan's fluid motions caused her heart to squeeze in her chest. He was an experienced lover now. The years spent apart hadn't been solitary ones for him.

She ceased to think as his mouth closed around the peak of her breast. He tugged gently and pulled the tightening nipple into the heat and moistness of his mouth. His tongue flicked over the tip. She writhed beneath him, and her hips moved in restless patterns against his. He molded her bottom in his hands and raised her into the cradle of his hips, holding her tightly against the hardness there.

The gentle tug of Logan's mouth on her breast sent shivers to the core of her body pressed against the steel strength of his.

Logan dragged his mouth back up to her lips, plunging his tongue into her mouth. Her eyes flew open at the shocking intensity of the act, as a loud crash of thunder outside rattled the windows. The candle flames flickered and danced. The storm had returned in all its fury.

His mouth plundered hers as his thumbs brushed over her aching nipples. She pulled her mouth away from his and gasped for breath. He kissed her neck, then took the hard peak of her breast into his mouth.

Her hands feathered over his back. Her nails scraped his skin when his teeth grazed her flesh. She gloried in his sudden indrawn breath when her fingers skimmed his tautened stomach muscles.

"It's been so long," he whispered shakily into the heat of her mouth.

Sharlie couldn't take any more. Trembling with need, she slid her hands between their bodies and unfastened the snap of his jeans. She'd never been so bold before, but shyness eluded her as she eased the zipper down so she could push the soft, worn denim over his legs. Logan assisted in removing his jeans, then divested her of her own. At last, their naked bodies lay entwined from head to toe.

She savored the contact. The years had changed his body from that of a boy into that of a man. Where his chest had once been smooth, the crisp, curling hairs tickled her senses. The boy's wiry strength had turned into the muscled contours that cradled her feminine curves so perfectly. The part of him nestled against her most intimate womanhood had changed as well. Logan was all man now.

He rolled her beneath him. Her hand stroked down his jaw. The slight abrasion of his whisker-roughened chin scraped her sensitive skin. He pressed a searing kiss into her palm, and slid his hand between their bodies. She was wet and slick and ready for him. With one quick thrust of his hips, he slid into her.

Sharlie wrapped her legs around him and rocked to the slow, steady pulse of his hips as Logan set a sensual rhythm. Spiraling ripples of pleasure curled throughout her body. Their tempo increased as the swells centered at the exact spot their bodies were joined until, with a flash of light behind her eyes that rivaled any lightning storm on Earth, she exploded, shivering and pulsing in his arms. Her breath came in small gasps as he shuddered over her. He cried out as his liquid fire coursed into her.

They lay tangled in each other's arms until Logan eased his weight from her body. He cradled her against his side and kissed the top of her head. "I never thought I'd ever hold you like this again." His voice wasn't steady yet.

Sharlie snuggled closer to him. Firelight danced over them, casting a rosy glow over their bare flesh. Logan reached for her chin, tilting her face up until she looked into his gleaming eyes. "I can't believe we're together again." He placed a hot, moist kiss on her upturned lips.

She opened her mouth, and his tongue dipped inside to touch hers. A shock wave raced through her body. It had always been like this. They'd never been able to get enough of each another.

She mimicked his action, thrusting her tongue into the warm recess of his mouth. She felt his instant reaction in the hardness that pressed against her thigh. She laughed in amazement. "You can't possibly. We just—"

With a fierce growl Logan rolled her beneath him again. His weight pressed her into the plush carpet. "Yes, we did and, yes, I can."

The sensual push of his hips against hers was all the proof she needed to know he was serious.

"I've been without you for far too long, and I intend to make up for lost time." His mouth swooped down to posses hers in another mind-numbing kiss.

They made love again in front of the fire, and later Logan carried her to his room and made love to her there. The storm that continued to rage outside was no match for the intensity of passionate lovers, reunited at last.

****

Hours later, as they once again lay spent in each others' arms Logan pulled Sharlie against his side. He kissed the top of her head and whispered, "This is a new beginning for us. With no more secrets to keep us apart."

Her heart stopped, then started again with a

painful thud. Logan's hand caressed the exact spot that had once held the baby they had made long ago. The baby he'd never known about. The only baby they could ever have.

She laid awake a long time after Logan's even breathing told her he had fallen asleep. She owed him the truth. He had a right to know about his baby. But how would he react? She blamed herself for the loss of their baby. Wouldn't he do the same?

She couldn't bear his anger, or the pain she was sure to see in his eyes if she told him. Wasn't it better to keep it from him? To spare him all that she'd suffered for twelve years? The past couldn't be changed.

One thing definitely hadn't changed.

She loved him.

It had taken her a while to admit it to herself. The beauty of what she felt was tinged with sadness because she could never tell Logan how she felt. Despite her feelings, they had no future together. He wanted a family, and she couldn't give him that.

She would settle for these fleeting, precious moments with him, and then let him go.

****

As dawn crept over the horizon, Logan watched Sharlie as she slept next to him on the wide bed. He still couldn't believe she was here with him like this. The constant fear that last night had been a wonderful, sensual dream had kept him up most of the night as he willed her not to disappear.

She murmured something in her sleep. Taking care not to wake her, he brushed an errant strand of blond hair away from her face. The silken texture slid through his fingers, evoking erotic memories of the night before.

Now that he had her back, he wasn't going to ever let her go. He couldn't wait to start their future together. To raise a family with her, just like they'd

117

planned all those years ago.

An image formed in his mind of a blond-haired, blue-eyed little girl cuddled in his arms. Of course their daughter would look just like Sharlie. Logan could see her walking hand in hand with a little boy who looked like him. Her belly swollen with a third child.

The vision was so real Logan had to blink his eyes several times before his bedroom came back into focus. Ever since he'd been eighteen he'd wanted a family with Sharlie. Soon, it would be more than a dream.

Before that could happen, he had one thing to settle. He wanted to find her father. His gut clenched at the thought of what Robert Montgomery had done to them. Last night he had told Sharlie it was in the past, but he couldn't let it go that easily. He had a few questions he needed answered.

Chapter Ten

Logan held Sharlie's hand later that day as they walked into The Corral. He leaned down to steal a quick kiss as Pete walked out of his office.

The older man took one look at them and grinned. "Well, I'll be damned. It's about time, I might add."

Logan smiled sheepishly and watched with pleasure as a faint blush stained Sharlie's cheeks.

"I have some work to do in my office," she said and winked at him.

He understood. His job was to keep Pete occupied so Sharlie and the rest of the staff could get things ready for the party later on that night. He couldn't resist placing another soft kiss on her lips, then watched the sway of her jean-clad hips as she walked away.

Erotic memories of those hips moving against his were interrupted by Pete's voice. "I hope your intentions are honorable, young man."

The other man's voice teased, but Logan understood the seriousness behind the words.

"Yes, sir, they are. I plan to marry Sharlie."

Pete looked pleased. "Good. Damn good."

Logan steered Pete toward his office. "But for right now, there are a few things you and I need to take care of concerning this bar."

****

Several hours later Logan walked down the stairs into the bar. His eyes scanned the room for Sharlie, his gaze moving past the colorful decorations to rest on her. She was talking to Zach,

119

her head bent close to his. He frowned, then forced himself to relax. Nothing was going on between the two of them. With studied nonchalance, he walked over to the pair.

Sharlie looked up and greeted him with the sweetest, sexiest smile he'd ever seen. The uncertainty of moments before vanished like dust on the wind. Zach's smile of greeting was a little more restrained, but held no animosity, only a resigned acceptance.

"Hi, sweetheart." Logan smiled down at her and kissed her cheek. He couldn't help it. He wanted to put his hands all over her. Last night had whetted his appetite for more.

"Hi, yourself." Sharlie's smile widened as a spark of awareness lit her eyes at the brief touch of his lips on her skin. The heated gleam was an answering match to Logan's need.

"We're all set down here. How do you think it looks? Are you sure Pete won't come down until it's time?"

He chuckled at the rapid fire of questions. His gaze traveled around the barroom. Streamers and balloons hung from every available surface. Several banners with the words GOOD-BYE, WE'LL MISS YOU, and HAPPY TRAILS hung from each bar as well. The cake they had ordered held a place of honor on one of the pool tables. A protective, colored plastic tablecloth covered the green felt.

"It looks wonderful." He hugged Sharlie close to his side. "You guys did a great job. And I'm sure Pete won't be down until we're ready for him. I've got Jake and Kate talking to him upstairs."

"Kate?" Zach questioned. "What happened to Janet?"

Sharlie laughed, and the sound rolled in pleasant waves over Logan. "Keep up, will you. That was weeks ago. You know Jake. He can't ever stay with one woman for long." She paused, looking at something across the room. "I need to take care of something. I'll be right back."

She left Logan standing with Zach. He didn't know what to say to him without Sharlie's buffering presence. They stood without speaking for a moment, each taking measure of the other.

"If you ever hurt her, you'll have to answer to me," Zach finally said, then turned on his heel, leaving Logan alone.

\*\*\*\*

"I think Pete was surprised," Sharlie said later that night.

The party had wound down, but a few guests remained.

Enjoying the feel of her in his arms as they danced, Logan took a moment to answer. "Yeah, I think he was. We make a great team." He looked into her blue eyes, loving the way the pupils dilated as he deliberately let his hand drift down over her hip to cup her derriere and haul her closer to him. He let her feel the evidence of his desire.

"Logan," she whispered in shock. Her voice trembled around his name.

"I want to take you home. Now." His harsh voice grated out from between his teeth.

"Yes."

He tugged her from the dance floor.

They made it to the parking lot before Sharlie spoke. "What about the bar?"

"I already talked to Zach and Jake. They're going to close for the night."

"You planned this," she accused.

"You bet I did. I'm very resourceful. Now get in the truck, woman."

She scrambled in.

Logan slid into the driver's side but, instead of starting the truck, he reached over and pulled

Sharlie into his arms. "I've been wanting to do this all night," he said against her mouth before covering it with his own.

He slipped his tongue between her lips. Her heat and moistness threatened to drown him. He groaned when she touched the tip of her tongue to his.

His fingers found the buttons of her shirt and undid the top few. His hand slipped inside to cup her soft, full breast. Through the lace of her bra, he stroked the nipple, which tightened in response. Sharlie's moan vibrated against his mouth.

He pulled away, his heart thundering in his chest. "I have to get you home," he said, his voice unsteady. He couldn't get enough of her. He felt like a sex-starved teenager.

Sharlie nodded.

Logan started the truck with an impatient twist of the key. The vehicle roared to life, and he threw it into gear.

He kept his eyes fixed on the road, his hands on the wheel. The sexy rustle of clothing as Sharlie buttoned her shirt nearly undid him. He swallowed and risked a glance at her. A mistake. The desire on her face was visible in the glow of the streetlights that shone into the cab as they sped toward his ranch.

Gravel spewed as he finally turned the truck into his driveway. Logan cut off the engine with a jerky movement. He turned to her and ran a hand along the back of her seat. "Did I ever mention these seats recline?"

Sharlie looked at him with a blank stare for a moment before understanding dawned in her eyes. "You can't be serious," she stammered as he threaded his fingers through her hair. The silky strands slid against his skin like a sensual caress.

"Oh, I'm serious," Logan whispered. His fingers moved from her hair to undo the buttons of her shirt.

He parted the soft cotton, then pulled the tails from her jeans. His knuckles brushed over the soft skin of her stomach. She sucked in her breath at the contact. Her lacy bra opened easily to his touch. His gaze roved over the smooth skin revealed to him, while his heart thundered a heavy beat in his chest.

He tore open the buttons of his own shirt and yanked it from his jeans. His leather belt slid through the denim loops. He tossed it into the back seat of the truck. The buckle clanked softly as it landed. His hat followed.

He moved over the dividing console and joined Sharlie in her bucket seat. She had watched his hurried movements in silence, the desire in her eyes matching his own.

"Aren't we a little old for this?" she asked as he reached for the lever to lower the seat into a reclining position.

In answer, he covered her mouth in a heated kiss, then stretched out in the seat next to her. Her breasts brushed his naked chest. He grunted at the intimate contact as his mouth devoured hers. With his thumbs, he brushed her nipples until they hardened into tight peaks. She moaned, writhing against him in the confining space.

"I can't wait," Logan groaned into her mouth.

Her nails dug into the skin of his back beneath his open shirt. Their harsh breathing filled the cab. He unfastened her jeans. "Lift your hips, honey. That's it," he whispered as Sharlie complied, and he slid the denim, along with her panties, down her legs. He unbuttoned his own jeans, then unzipped them to free himself from the crushing tightness.

"Yes, oh, Logan, please," Sharlie begged. Her hands kneaded the muscles in his back.

His hand stroked down her thigh, then inward, finding her moist heat. He shifted, parting her legs with his knee. He pressed forward until he filled her, closing his mouth over hers to absorb the sigh of pleasure that escaped her as they joined.

He rocked against her. The rhythm pushed him deeper into the tight warmth of her body. She quivered in his arms, then contracted around him, shuddering and whimpering as ecstasy claimed her. He pushed himself into her one last time. His own release crashed over him, and he called her name. His shudders mirrored hers, and his pulse pounded in his veins.

With a trembling hand, Logan smoothed a strand of hair away from Sharlie's forehead. "That sure brings back memories."

Sharlie laughed. "Doesn't it seem like we used to have more room?" Her uneven breath stirred the damp, tight curls on his chest.

"Yeah, I guess we've grown up a bit since the last time we made love in my truck. Kind of a shame, don't you think?" Logan chuckled in regret, then kissed her before moving away in the limited space allowed. "I guess we'd better get in the house," he added reluctantly.

"At least you don't have to take me back to my father's house tonight."

Logan grinned. "I guess there are some advantages to being grown up."

****

Sharlie cuddled next to Logan under the warm covers of his bed. She loved waking up in his arms. Her heart ached at the thought of putting an end to it. Which is what she needed to do.

Either that or she had to tell him everything. She couldn't keep leading him on. Being here like this with him was selfish. Deep down she knew she shouldn't have let things get this far. Trouble was, it felt so right being with him again. When he touched her, all rational thought fled, and she gave into the temptation of the pleasure he promised. The years apart had been lonely. She'd missed him.

She'd have to make a choice. Break it off with Logan and keep her secret, or confess what she'd done with their baby.

Both led to certain heartbreak.

Logan stirred and placed a kiss in her hair.

"Hey, sleepyhead," she teased.

"Hey, yourself."

He rolled away from her to sit on the side of the bed. Her eyes were drawn to the sexy play of muscles in his back as he stretched. "You hungry?" He looked at her over his shoulder.

"I should be getting home."

"Oh." Logan's tone reflected his disappointment.

"I have some things I need to do before work tonight," Sharlie explained, hating the look on his face and shuddering at the thought of how he'd look if she told him they couldn't see each other anymore.

They dressed in silence.

"Are you sure you can't stay?" Logan asked as he walked her to the door.

"No, I'm sorry. I'll see you tonight at the bar."

He shook his head. "I won't be in for a couple of days. I need to go out of town."

Although disappointment flooded through Sharlie at his words, putting some distance between them was a good idea at this point. The longer she let herself be involved with Logan, the harder it would be to end it.

She paused in the doorway. "When will you be back?"

"Two or three days. I'm not sure." He kissed her softly. "When I get back, we need to have a talk."

Sharlie's heart skipped a beat, and her breath caught in her throat. "Wh...what about?"

"What we're going to do with the rest of our lives."

"The rest of our lives?" Sharlie felt like she'd

been punched in the gut. He couldn't be thinking about the future. They didn't have one.

****

Later, alone in her apartment, the words echoed through Sharlie's mind. What was she going to do? Logan wanted to talk about their future.

Her soul ached, because more than anything she wanted to have one with him.

She dragged a chair from the kitchen into her bedroom. From the top shelf of her closet, way in the back, she retrieved a small box. The lid was coated with a thick layer of dust. The fine particles caused her to sneeze when she blew them away. Her heart pounded in her chest as she carried the box to the bed. With trembling fingers, she lifted the lid and stared at the precious items inside.

A tiny hospital bracelet lay atop a stack of photos. Although she hadn't looked at the pictures in years, she could see the images in her mind. Tears flowed freely down her cheeks as she flipped through the memories in front of her.

They were a chronicle of her time with Logan. The last one showed them at her graduation. A few months later she would have turned eighteen and been free of her father. Their smiles were wide and their eyes filled with hope for the future.

She'd been pregnant already, but hadn't known it yet.

Soon after, Logan had left, and Sharlie's life had taken its devastating turn.

She picked up the bracelet, imagining for a moment she could feel the tiny fingers of the baby who had worn it grasp her own.

What would happen if she told Logan the truth? Could he find it in his heart to forgive her for robbing them of their only chance to have a child? Could he accept her the way she was and give up his desire to have a family?

Her thoughts, as they often did, drifted back to the bittersweet time of the birth, the time she had spent in the hospital afterward, and the toll it had taken on her life. The guilt she felt over her baby weighed on her mind and in her heart. If she and Logan were going to have any chance at a future together, didn't he have a right to know? He should hear the facts from her, not some clinical doctor.

Somehow she needed to find the courage to tell him everything when he returned. If he hated her for what she had done and walked away, it would be only what she deserved. One more heartbreak to add to the burden she already carried. Maybe there was a chance he would understand and forgive her. But she loved him too much to keep the truth from him any longer.

****

Logan sucked in a deep breath and walked up the stairs leading to the imposing front door of Robert Montgomery's Connecticut home. Like the one Sharlie had grown up in, the house was sprawling and elegant, designed to show off the wealth of the man who lived there.

He smiled grimly, wishing he were back home holding Sharlie in his arms. He didn't know what he was going to say to her father. He wasn't the white trash boy Robert Montgomery had seen him as all those years ago. Back then Sharlie's father hadn't wanted Logan around his little girl. Now Logan was the man who intended to marry that girl. Childish as it seemed, he wanted to throw Robert Montgomery's failure to keep them apart right in his arrogant face.

He felt inside his jacket pocket, the reassuring shape of the ring box a reminder that he and Sharlie were going to spend the rest of their lives together. He couldn't wait to marry her, have a family with her, grow old with her.

First, he wanted, no needed, to confront the man who had kept them apart for so long.

He took one final cleansing breath and rang the bell. To his surprise the door was opened by Robert Montgomery himself. Logan quelled the instant surge of anger the sight of the man induced.

Sharlie's father looked much older than the last time he'd seen him. His hair had more gray in it than brown, and a tiredness resided in his eyes. "Robert Montgomery?"

"Yes?" The man studied Logan with a puzzled frown.

"Surely I haven't changed that much in twelve years."

Recognition dawned in the older man's gaze, and his eyes narrowed. "Well, I'll be damned. I didn't think I'd ever see you again." His tone implied he was sorry to see him now. His gaze traveled to the porch behind Logan, and for a moment he looked disappointed. "Sharlina's not with you?"

"Why would Sharlie be with me? If I recall, at our last meeting, you paid me to get out of her life."

The gray haired man's eyes glinted dangerously as his gaze slid down the well-tailored, and expensive, suit Logan wore. "I see you've done quite well with that money."

Logan held his temper in check. "I never spent a dime of your money." He could see from the look in the other man's eyes that he didn't believe him. Apparently the man had so much money, an uncashed check for twenty-five-thousand dollars went unnoticed.

"What do you want? Are you looking for another handout, Reed? You must be damned desperate for money to track me down out here after all this time."

Logan curbed the impulse to shove his fist into the other man's gloating face. "Actually, I'm looking for some answers. I want to know why you did it?"

128

Robert Montgomery didn't pretend to misunderstand. "I didn't think you were good enough for my daughter. I still don't. But considering how things worked out, I never had a choice in the matter." His laugh was harsh. "Ironic isn't it? You wound up with my money and my daughter."

Logan didn't correct him again. Not a cent of the money had been touched. But uneasiness stirred in the back of his mind. How had her father known that he and Sharlie were together? In fact, he had asked earlier if she were with Logan. Why would he have asked that? Something wasn't right.

Logan ignored the disturbing feelings and addressed the man's comment. "It wasn't your choice to make."

"No, I guess it wasn't." For a moment there was genuine regret in the man's voice, but then the steel edge was back. "I wanted better things for my daughter. She deserved better than to be strapped to a good-for-nothing like you raising a passel of brats. I told her when she came to me looking for help if she went after you, she wasn't welcome back in my house. She made her choice. Sharlina shouldn't be expecting any handouts from me either."

Logan's mind reeled. What had stopped Sharlie from coming after him? And what had she needed help with? He wanted to pummel the man standing before him for treating his own flesh and blood with such cruelty. His stomach churned. Hidden meanings lurked behind Robert Montgomery's words.

"We don't need your handouts." Logan turned on his heel to go. It had been a mistake to come. Instead of the answers he sought, he had found more questions.

"You couldn't keep your hands off my daughter, could you? How many brats have you saddled her with by now? Because I'm sure you didn't have enough sense to stop after the first one."

The words stopped Logan dead in his tracks. His heart gave a sickening lurch as he turned back to face Sharlie's father. "The first one?"

The other man snorted. "Stop playing games, Reed. Sharlina told me she was pregnant before she set off to find you."

Logan felt the color drain from his face, and he had to grab the porch rail for support. "Sharlie was pregnant?"

"You didn't know?"

Logan could only shake his head. He was sure his shock was written all over his face. He felt numb.

Robert Montgomery smiled in triumph, all traces of regret gone. He was a man who wanted to control those around him and usually succeeded. "Well, then, I guess she took my advice after all and got rid of your bastard before it became a burden on society. Remember, Reed, I always win." The door slammed in Logan's face.

Logan hardly noticed. His entire world had crashed down around him.

Chapter Eleven

Dismay filled Sharlie when she pulled into Logan's driveway and saw his truck sitting there. She had planned to be there when he arrived home. Hoping against hope he'd understand what she had to tell him, she'd stopped at the grocery store and picked up a few things for dinner.

A quick glance at her watch told her she wasn't late. He must have taken an earlier flight.

Which was fine with her. The last two days without him had seemed like an eternity. She couldn't wait to see him, and although she was nervous about what she needed to tell him, in her heart she knew she was doing the right thing.

Maybe he would understand.

Taking a deep breath, she headed up the steps. She pushed open the front door, calling as she did so, "Logan?"

He was sitting on the couch in front of the unlit fireplace. Excitement coursed through her. "You're home early. Did you have a nice trip? I'm so glad to see you. Let me put these things in the kitchen first, but then there's something I need to talk to you about."

On the way back from the kitchen she realized he hadn't said a word. He remained motionless, staring at the empty fireplace. A chill of foreboding snaked down her spine as she approached the couch.

"Logan?"

He looked up at her, but Sharlie wished he hadn't. His eyes were cold, like glaciers, and they cut deeply into her. The icy chill grabbed her heart.

She reached out a tentative hand to him, repeating his name.

"Don't touch me." His hard voice matched the look in his eyes.

She froze.

"I went to see your father," Logan continued, his voice flat, controlled.

"My father?" She sank down onto the nearby chair, her strength deserting her.

"How could you?" He bit off the words.

He knew. Her worst nightmare had come true. "Please," she begged through trembling lips. "Let me explain."

"Explain?" The control slipped from Logan's voice. He rose from the couch to tower over her. "I think it's a little too late for explanations, don't you?"

"I was going to tell you, I swear it. I was going to tell you tonight," Sharlie half whispered. Tears coursed down her cheeks.

"Don't play games with me. How in the hell were you going to explain that you were pregnant with my child and never bothered to tell me? And how did you plan on explaining where that child is?"

The anger and hatred in Logan's eyes were far worse than the dead calm of minutes ago. Her heart beat a painful rhythm in her chest, and she was unable to speak around the sobs gathering in her throat.

He looked at her for a long moment, then turned away as if he couldn't stand the sight of her anymore. He paused before walking out of the room. "I don't think you can offer me any explanation that would make me understand what you did to my child." He strode from the room. The back door slammed.

Sharlie's heart shattered into a million pieces.

First one sob, then another tore from her throat. Her soul would never recover from the heartbreak of losing Logan again. Knowing the fault rested with her made it harder to bear.

She should have told him right from the beginning. True, he would have reacted the same way, but at least she would have saved herself the pain of having opened her heart to him again.

Through a haze of tears Sharlie looked around the room that had become so familiar to her in a few short days. She didn't belong there. She had no place in Logan's home, or his life.

Ineffectively wiping the tears from her eyes, she rose from the chair on unsteady legs and left the house, shutting the door behind her with a soft click. She sat in her car and stared at the house. This time all of her dreams were gone for sure. She wouldn't have a third chance to make things right with Logan.

Her trembling fingers managed to start the ignition. The ranch faded into the darkness as she drove down the gravel driveway. She was leaving more than a house behind. She was leaving everything. Logan, The Corral, her friends, her entire life. This was the moment she'd been dreading ever since Logan had walked back into her life. She had known it would come to this. As surely as she knew the blame rested entirely on her shoulders.

****

Logan was more than halfway toward getting completely drunk when the doorbell rang. He considered ignoring it, but the person at the door was persistent.

"Go away," he roared when the bell pealed again. "Son of a bi—" Logan bit off the curse and stalked to the door, yanking it open.

Pete stood there. He took in Logan's unkempt appearance and frowned in disapproval at the half-empty tumbler in his hand.

Logan downed the remaining liquid in the glass, welcoming the burning path it seared down his throat to his belly. "What are you doing here?" he growled.

"Mind if I come in?"

"I'm not in the mood for company." He attempted to shut the door.

The other man ignored him and walked into the family room. He nodded his head at the glass clutched in Logan's hand. "Keeping company with the likes of that isn't the way to solve your problems, you know."

Logan laughed without mirth and followed Pete into the room. "Yeah, well it's a damn sight better than thinking about them."

"Sharlie came to see me a little while ago."

"I don't want to talk about her."

"She was upset," Pete continued as though he hadn't heard.

"Look, Pete," Logan warned. "I know you mean well, but I'm telling you, I don't want to talk about Sharlie." Saying her name sent a fresh wave of pain crashing over him. He poured himself another drink from the bottle sitting on the end table.

"She told me she was leaving town."

"So?"

"So you need to stop her."

Logan downed the contents of his glass. "What makes you think I want her to stay?"

"Because she also told me what happened, and I think you're acting like a jackass."

"What?" Logan couldn't believe what he was hearing. "Obviously you didn't hear the correct version of the story, or you wouldn't be saying that."

"Oh, I heard the right version alright," Pete said. "I'm wondering if you did."

The liquor was finally doing its job. Pete wasn't

making any sense. "I know what I heard."

"Did you give her a chance to explain?"

"Explain?"

"Yeah, did you give her a chance to tell her side?"

"Her side?" He sounded like an idiot repeating everything Pete said, but the man was making no sense. "There aren't two sides to this. Sharlie was pregnant, but there's no baby. She got rid of my baby." Pain laced the harsh words.

"Did she tell you that?"

"She didn't deny it."

"But did she tell you that?" Pete persisted.

"Her father told me," Logan ground out.

Pete smiled, but the expression held no humor. "Ah, yes, the man who tried to buy you out of his daughter's life. The man who turned his own daughter away when he found out she was pregnant. A reliable source."

It took a moment for Pete's words to sink into Logan's drink muddled brain. "What are you trying to say?"

Pete sighed, but continued. "Look, Sharlie didn't tell me everything. But I do know that little lady pretty well, and I'm telling you, she would never get rid of a baby. Not in the way you're thinking."

Logan sank down on the couch, his legs refusing to hold him up anymore. How could he be wrong? Sharlie had been pregnant. She'd admitted as much. But could he be wrong about what happened to the baby? Pete was right. Logan knew her better than that.

The thought sobered him. He groaned, remembering the awful things he'd said to her.

"I have to find her." He surged to his feet. It took a moment to steady himself.

"You'd best sober up before you get into that truck of yours. Won't do any good to go driving around town in your condition. Likely to get yourself killed, and that won't be helpin' Miss Sharlie none."

Logan nodded. Pete's advice was sound. "I will." He walked the older man to the door. He paused and laid a hand on his shoulder. "Thank you for coming over here tonight."

"You're welcome."

After Pete left, Logan started the automatic coffee maker. He jumped into an icy shower. The freezing water soon cleared his senses, but did little to clear the muddled thoughts that raced through his mind.

Where was Sharlie? What had happened to their baby? She would never forgive him for the awful things he'd said to her. Hell, he didn't deserve her forgiveness, but he would ask for it anyway.

After the shower, Logan gulped a steaming cup of coffee. He needed to find her, but didn't have a clue where to begin. He decided to try the obvious place first, although he didn't hold much hope of finding her at her apartment.

In a short time Logan pulled his pickup into the parking lot of Sharlie's complex. He scanned the cars in the crowded lot, but didn't see her familiar compact. He tried the buzzer first, in a vain attempt to reach her, then fished her key out of his pocket. He unlocked the building door, then let himself in to her apartment.

"Sharlie?" He hadn't expected an answer, but disappointment coursed through him when there was no reply.

"Where are you?" he whispered to the emptiness surrounding him.

He looked around the apartment, searching for a clue as to what to do next. He had to find her. Find her and beg her to forgive him.

He only hoped it wasn't too late.

****

The tires on his truck squealed as he pulled into the parking lot of The Corral. He was desperate enough to ask Zach for help. He had no idea what time it was, but the empty lot told him the bar hadn't opened for the night yet. Right now business was the last thing on his mind.

He barreled through the front doors, but stopped short as Zach emerged from a nearby office. "Zach, I need—"

"You bastard." Zach's fist shot out, catching Logan with a viscous uppercut to the jaw.

Logan's head snapped back and the world spun. The salty taste of blood filled his mouth.

When his vision cleared, Zach stood before him, a murderous look in his eyes.

Before either man could say a word, Jake appeared in the hallway. "Cool it, Zach. This isn't helping Sharlie."

"It's making me feel a hell of a lot better."

"I need to find her," Logan said.

"Why? So you can hurt her again?" Zach's angry stance remained.

"So I can tell her how sorry I am and beg her to forgive me," Logan replied levelly.

Zach seemed taken aback by his candor. "Don't you think it's a little late for apologies?"

Logan closed his eyes for a brief moment. "God, I hope not," he breathed. "I can't lose her." He looked at Zach, unashamed to let the other man hear the desperation in his voice. "I have to find her. You're the only one who can help me."

"What makes you think I'd help you after what you did to her?"

He wasn't sure how much Zach knew, but he had a gut feeling the other man could help him find Sharlie. He took a chance and laid his heart on the line. "I know how you feel about me, and I know I don't deserve your help. But Sharlie's out there somewhere, hurting like hell because of me, and I have to try to make it right. I love her.

"I'll do it, with or without your help, but it'll be a hell of a lot quicker with it. The faster I find her, the sooner I can try to make things right." Logan paused. "Isn't that what we both want? For Sharlie to stop hurting?"

The indecision reflected in the other man's eyes prompted him to go on. "If I can't make things right, I'll walk away. Sharlie can come back here to you." He prayed his words were getting through. Too much time had been wasted already. "If she doesn't want me anymore, I promise you, I'll leave here." A stab of pain, like a knife, twisted into him at the thought of not seeing her again.

Zach eyed him warily. "You bought this place."

"I'll sell it," Logan vowed with conviction. He could tell Zach was wavering, so he pressed on. "Please, do you know where she is?"

"I hope I'm not going to regret this," Zach muttered. "I don't know for sure, but I have an idea where she might be."

\*\*\*\*

"Zach said I might find you here."

Sharlie jumped at Logan's words. The faint noise of the small stream had muffled his approach. She sat on a log, staring out over the trickling water. After leaving Pete's house, she had driven around for hours, not knowing where to go, only knowing she had to escape.

"You must be freezing."

She was cold. The gray sky threatened an early season snow.

His boots crunched in the fallen leaves as he drew nearer. His warmth and the spicy scent that enveloped her when he placed his jacket around her shoulders threatened to start another avalanche of tears.

The silence stretched between them until she couldn't stand it any longer. "Why are you here, Logan?"

"I've been looking for you all day." He paused. "I'm so sorry. So sorry I hurt you." His voice caught, and he cleared his throat before continuing. "Please forgive me. I don't want to lose you again."

The words rolled over Sharlie. She took them in and held them close to her bruised heart. Could she forgive him? The words soothing her battered soul told her she could. But would he ever forgive her?

He came to stand beside her.

She glanced up at him. He looked haggard and worn. A bruise marred his jaw, and there was a cut in his lower lip.

"What happened?"

"It's nothing," Logan said.

"Did you get into a fight?"

"Zach wasn't too happy that I upset you."

"Zach hit you?" Sharlie asked in shock.

"I deserved it. Look, I didn't come here to talk about Zach."

He turned away to stare out over the moving water. "I went to see your father because I wanted to ask him who the hell he thought he was, messing with our lives. I wanted him to know his plan hadn't worked. We were together in spite of what he'd done to keep us apart. Together where we belonged, even if it had taken us a while to get there." Logan paused and laughed. The bitter sound echoed in the stillness. "I got taken in again. I'm not a naive teenager anymore, but I fell for his lies just the same."

Logan's voice grew harsher as he spoke, and she could hear the tears clogging his throat. An answering drop of moisture escaped from the corner of her eye and rolled down her cheek. What else had her father told him?

Almost as if hearing her unspoken words, Logan turned toward her, then glanced away. He raised his face to the sky, as if looking for the strength to go on. "He told me you had an abortion. I believed him."

Silence thundered in Sharlie's ears after the whispered confession. Her heart thudded in her chest.

"You thought I had an abortion?" The broken whisper of her voice hung in the sudden stillness. Even nature held its breath.

His gaze returned to hers. "Yes."

She read the pain in his eyes. Pain that matched her own. "How could you think that?"

Logan lowered his gaze. "Your father told me—"

Sharlie's laugh was brittle, unnatural. "I think you've played that card before. You can't blame my father for this one."

"Please," Logan begged. "I didn't know what to think."

"So you thought the worst."

Guilt flooded Logan's eyes.

Part of her wanted to throw herself into his arms and make everything right again. But he had hurt her too badly. How could he think something so awful? Her heart felt like it had been ripped apart. She had regrets about what she'd done, but she would have never destroyed their child.

"I'm sorry," he whispered.

"I know you are. I'm not sure that's good enough."

She turned and walked away without a backward glance.

Sharlie had just turned the key in the ignition when the first snowflake hit the windshield. She stilled, remembering another time she'd run away in a snowstorm. She'd allowed her emotions to rule common sense that time, and she'd lost everything.

No, she hadn't had an abortion, but the end

result was the same. Their baby was gone, and they wouldn't have the chance for another one.

The need to escape from the car overwhelmed her. Logan caught up to her as she was stepping out of the driver's door.

He reached to touch her, but stopped before he did and shoved his hands in his pockets. He looked as if he were trying to read her thoughts.

"I know I have no right to ask for your forgiveness. I said cruel and terrible things to you. But I'm sorry. Don't let the fact that I was an idiot to believe your father cheat us out of any more time together. I know you didn't get rid of our baby."

His anguished plea tore through Sharlie, stripping away the tight control she had on her emotions. They broke free in a strangled sob. "But I did get rid of our baby. Don't you understand? It's my fault our baby is gone."

Chapter Twelve

Logan's face froze in shock, and then he took her shoulders in his hands. "Don't you think it's time we talked about what happened?"

Shadows of pain still lurked in his eyes, but his soft words caressed Sharlie like a warm breeze.

He was right. They needed to talk.

"Yes."

The warmth in his gaze almost made her forget about the chill in the air. But as the snow fell in earnest, she shivered despite the jacket he'd tossed over her shoulders.

"Not here, though. You're freezing. Follow me to my house?"

Sharlie nodded, then got back in her car. Her fingers trembled as she started the ignition, then put the car in gear. She didn't know what to say to Logan, but the time had come for him to know the truth.

About everything.

****

The drive to the ranch didn't take long. Sharlie settled in the corner of the sofa in the cozy family room. She twisted a strand of hair around her finger.

Logan built a fire, then turned to face her. "Are you warming up?"

"I'm fine." As fine as she could be while the weight of what she had to tell him rested on her guilty heart. Not a day went by that she didn't think about the decision she'd made and what had happened afterwards. But she'd never spoken to anyone about it. How could she find the words to tell

Logan?

"Do you want anything?"

She desperately wanted to retreat to the security of his embrace, but knew she'd never get the words out if he touched her. "No, I...I just don't know where to start."

He nodded, then sat down in the chair, his arms resting on his knees. The casual pose belied the tension emanating from him. It matched her own. What would happen once he knew the truth? She couldn't bear to see the look of hatred in his eyes again. But it was far past time to tell him.

She rose and went to stand before the fire, staring into the flames, but not seeing them.

"When I found out I was pregnant, I didn't know what to do. You'd already left, and I didn't know where you were. I thought I could convince my father to help me find you."

She glanced over her shoulder at Logan. "Pretty stupid, huh?" Her laugh was bitter. "I should have known better. Of course he wouldn't help me. He said he'd have you arrested if you ever showed your face again. Then he told me to get rid of the baby. To have an abortion." She paused, fighting for composure. The memory of her father's words still had the power to cause pain.

"Bastard," Logan muttered under his breath.

"I never realized how much he hated you until then." She risked a glance at him. "Even though you'd left me, or so I thought, I knew you would want to know about the baby. I figured we could work something out. I told my father I was going to find you. He said if that's what I wanted, I shouldn't bother coming back ever again."

She sensed Logan was about to say something and turned to face him. "Please, let me finish." She hadn't gotten to the hard parts yet.

"I went to your mom's apartment first, but she

didn't know where you'd gone. Or if she did, she wasn't telling."

Logan shook his head. "I didn't tell her."

"After that I got in my car and started driving. Snow was falling hard. The roads were covered, and it was icy." She hugged herself to ward off the chill the memory brought back, the heat of the fire not enough to warm her. "I should have waited until the storm stopped, but I needed to find you. I wasn't thinking straight." Sharlie kept her voice flat, trying to stem the flood of emotions racing through her. Her palms were sweaty despite the chill that lingered.

"I...I took a curve too fast and the car slid. I lost control and went into a ditch. The cramps started almost right away. By the time the paramedics got there I was bleeding." Her voice trembled and her heart pounded in her chest. A tear rolled down her cheek. "So much blood," she whispered. "I thought...I thought our baby was gone." Her tear-filled gaze sought Logan's. "I thought I had killed our baby."

He rose from the chair in one fluid motion and crossed to her. He gathered her shuddering form into his arms and held her, smoothing his hands down her back. His body trembled as he held her close and murmured soft, soothing words into her hair.

She clung to him, but couldn't bask in his comfort for too long. She needed to tell him the rest.

After another moment she pulled away. She walked a few steps from him, staring into the fire once again while she gathered her thoughts.

"I was in the hospital for a while. I had a couple of broken ribs and a concussion."

"And the baby?" Logan's voice was hoarse.

She forced herself to go on. "The baby was fine. But as I lay there all that time I realized I could never be a good mother to it. As much as I already loved it, I knew it deserved a better life than I'd ever be able to give it."

"That's not—" Logan began.

"So I gave it up for adoption." There. The words were out. She hardly dared to breathe. What would he say now that knew? He'd never be able to forgive her. She'd never forgiven herself.

"You gave our baby up for adoption?"

Sharlie nodded.

Silence filled the room.

Logan stood, not moving, not saying a word. His expression gave no hint to his thoughts.

Finally, Sharlie couldn't stand it anymore. "Please, say something." She had to know what he was thinking.

"I don't know what to say."

Sharlie nodded. Although she had hoped differently, she shouldn't have expected Logan to understand or forgive her for what she'd done. She took a deep breath and willed herself not to cry. Time enough for that later.

"I should leave. I'm sorry, Logan. Truly I am." Nothing else she said would change a thing. Nothing could bring their baby back to them.

She headed for the door, but his words stopped her.

"Don't go."

She turned back. Tears coursed down her cheeks when he came to her. He drew her into his embrace. A shuddering breath escaped her as he placed a soft kiss in her hair.

"Look at me."

His command reached her ears, but she couldn't face him. She shook her head against his chest.

"Look at me, Sharlie," he repeated. He tilted her chin up.

To Sharlie's surprise, his eyes weren't filled with hatred.

"I'm so sorry."

The words caught her off guard. "What?"

"I'm so sorry I wasn't there with you. I'm so sorry you had to make that decision alone."

"I thought you'd hate me for what I did."

"You were incredibly brave."

"But I gave our baby away." Sharlie's fear of Logan's anger was so ingrained, she had trouble adjusting to the deep compassion and understanding in his voice.

"You did what was right for you at the time."

"If only I hadn't rushed out into the storm. Knowing that I almost killed our baby with my recklessness—"

"It was an accident. You were upset. People don't think rationally when they're upset. I should know," he added in a self-depreciating tone. "I believed your father the other day, and I believed him about that check all those years ago. I know you'd never say or do something like that."

Sharlie considered Logan's words. She had believed he'd asked her father for the check. If they could believe such awful things about each other, maybe they weren't meant to be together.

Logan must have read her mind. "We were teenagers. We both made mistakes because we didn't know any better."

"What about now?"

"I was an ass."

Sharlie almost laughed. Having shared part of her burden with Logan, her heart felt lighter, but she had to be sure. "You forgive me?" If he understood about the adoption, maybe he'd be able to accept what else she had to tell him.

"There's nothing to forgive. Please stop blaming yourself about the baby. It wasn't meant to be for us at the time. We both had some growing up to do." He pulled her into his arms again.

Sharlie nodded against the solid wall of his chest. The steady beat of his heart sounded beneath her ear. How she had longed for his comfort and strength all those years ago.

"She was beautiful."

Logan's arms tightened. "We had a girl?"

Sharlie pushed away to look up into his eyes, which were filled with tears. She nodded. "I..." She didn't know what else to say.

After a moment, Logan spoke. "I know you made some couple very happy by giving them our baby. I bet they love her more than anything in the world."

He lifted Sharlie's chin so their gazes once again locked. "I don't know why things happened the way they did. But I do know this, if you give me the chance, I'll give you lots more babies."

Pain started in her heart and spread until the ache filled her entire body. As hard as it had been to tell him about giving their baby up for adoption, there was something else he needed to know. He couldn't give her any more babies.

She dug down deep inside herself for every ounce of courage she possessed. "Logan, I—"

He kissed her tenderly, cutting her off, then released her and went to the jacket he'd tossed on the chair when they'd come in. He opened a small velvet box and removed a sparkling diamond ring.

He returned and dropped to one knee before her. "I did go to Connecticut to see your father, but I also went to find this for you." He held up the solitaire with shaking fingers. "I love you, Sharlie. I always have, and I always will. No one's ever been in my heart besides you. I want to spend the rest of my life with you. Raise a family with you. Grow old with you. Will you marry me?"

She stared at the ring until tears blurred it from sight.

She blinked and looked down into his earnest

face. Once she would have given anything to hear those words from him. Now they only teased her with a fleeting glimpse of what could never be. He deserved more than she could give him.

She took a deep breath. "No."

Logan's face registered his shock. "What?"

"I...I'm sorry." She touched his face, one final touch to last a lifetime. "These past few days with you have been wonderful. More wonderful than I ever could have imagined." Her voice caught, but she struggled on. "I can't marry you. You deserve better than me." Tears obscured her vision again. Blindly, she turned from him and ran to the front door.

"Sharlie?"

She wrenched open the door, stumbling down the porch steps to her car.

Logan appeared in the doorway as she shifted into gear.

She saw his lips form her name, but she couldn't hear over the painful thump of her heart. For the second time in as many days, she drove away from his house.

This time she didn't look back.

****

Dumbfounded, Logan stared down the driveway long after Sharlie's taillights had disappeared. An icy wind tore at his hair and clothes, but it was no match for the chill surrounding his heart.

He looked at the ring clenched in his fingers. She'd said no. He couldn't believe it.

After they'd finally confessed all their secrets, he thought they were ready to move on and start a life together.

Why didn't Sharlie want to marry him?

He'd ached when she'd told him she'd given up their baby for adoption. The loss of their daughter saddened him, but the hurt was for Sharlie, who had let the guilt over her decision haunt her all these years. He'd been taken aback when she told him, but he understood why she'd done it. At seventeen, being a single mother would have been a scary prospect. It didn't mean he didn't want a life with her now. He loved her and wanted to give her more children.

He closed his hand around the ring.

He'd give her some time, but apparently there were still things they needed to talk about.

****

Not knowing where else to go, Sharlie drove to Zach's apartment. A glance at her watch told her he'd probably be at work, but she couldn't go home to her empty apartment. Logan would look for her there, and she couldn't face him.

She let herself in with the key Zach kept hidden on top of a light in the hallway, then collapsed on the couch.

Logan had proposed. It had taken everything in her to refuse. The look on his face would be ingrained in her memory forever.

Not marrying Logan was for the best. She wouldn't be a good wife. She couldn't give him the family he desperately wanted.

He would be okay. He'd get over her rejection and find someone else. Someone who would give him lots of children.

Fresh tears sprang to her eyes, surprising Sharlie. She thought she was all cried out.

She pulled the blanket from the back of the couch over herself as she lay down. Gradually her tears subsided, and emotionally exhausted, she drifted off.

****

"Sharlie?" The sound of her name and a gentle touch on her shoulder brought her awake.

She opened her eyes and slowly focused on Zach's face. "What time is it?"

"Three."

"Oh." It took a moment for the cobwebs to clear from her brain. "I must have fallen asleep." She pushed away the tangled blanket, then sat up.

Zach joined her on the couch. "What are you doing here?"

"Logan proposed."

"Oh." His voice mirrored his confusion.

"I said no."

"What?"

"I said no," Sharlie repeated. A tear slid down her cheek.

Zach stared at her and shook his head. "I don't understand."

"I can't marry Logan."

"Did he do something to you again?" Zach's voice was sharp. "When I told him where to find you I warned him—"

"He didn't do anything. It's me." She rose to pace the room. "We finally talked. About things we should have talked about a long time ago. But before I could tell him everything, he proposed."

Sharlie looked at Zach, then away again. "I can't marry him. I can't marry anyone. No one would want me if they knew."

Zach rose. He turned her to face him. "You're not making any sense. Any man in his right mind would want to marry you."

"Not if they knew."

"Knew what?" When she didn't respond, he shook her gently. "Talk to me, Sharlie."

She pulled out of his hold and turned away. "It doesn't matter." She couldn't bear to see the pity in Zach's eyes if she told him.

"Sharlie."

"Can I stay here tonight?"

"Of course, but why aren't you at your place?"

"Logan might look for me there."

"Why don't you want to see him? I'm sure he'd

understand whatever it is you have to tell him."

She shrugged.

"Fine. I won't bug you about it anymore. But for the record, I think you need to talk to him." He shook out the blanket she'd tossed aside. "I'll take the couch. You can have the bed."

"No, that's okay, I'll sleep out here."

Zach laid down, pulling the blanket up to his chin. "Too late. I was here first." He closed his eyes.

"Thanks, Zach." She kissed him on the forehead.

In his bedroom, she slipped into one of Zach's T-shirts, then slid under the covers.

Sleep eluded her as she lay there in the dark.

How many times had she dreamed about Logan proposing? Too many to count. In those dreams she never said no. But real life wasn't a dream. Real life was cold reality. And in reality, Logan wouldn't want to be married to her.

After what seemed like hours, she finally fell into a restless sleep.

****

She woke to the sound of voices in the living room. A glance at the bedside clock told her it was mid-morning. Who could Zach be talking to? After a shift at the bar, he usually wasn't up at this hour.

It didn't take her long to identify the deep timbre of Logan's voice.

What was he doing here? She wasn't ready to face him. After everything that had happened yesterday, she couldn't bear to tell him the truth. Her courage had deserted her.

He'd want an explanation, though. He'd want to know why she'd said no.

She needed to do something drastic to put an end to it once and for all.

Looking around Zach's bedroom, it suddenly hit her. If Logan thought she were with Zach, he wouldn't want to have anything to do with her.

151

She had nothing left to lose at this point. Logan owned The Corral. She wouldn't be going back there. Everything in her life would be different now, even her friendship with Zach.

Still dressed in nothing but Zach's T-shirt, she walked out of the bedroom. "Zach, are you coming back to bed?"

Two pairs of shocked eyes found hers.

Zach's mouth dropped open, while Logan's compressed into a tight line. His eyes flashed with heated emotion. Without a word, he turned and walked out the door.

Zach stood frozen in place as Sharlie approached. She held out her hand in a placating gesture. "I'm sorry."

His gaze slid down her body, then darted quickly away. "What the hell, Sharlie?"

"I'm sorry," she said again. "I had to find a way to make Logan see we couldn't be together."

A muscle twitched in Zach's cheek. "So you made it look like we're sleeping together?" A touch of hurt tinged his voice.

"I can't face him anymore," she tried to explain. "He won't want to talk to me now."

"No, I suppose not."

Sharlie cursed. She hadn't meant to hurt Zach.

He turned away. "I'm sure Logan won't go to your place, but if you still don't want to go home, you can stay here as long as you like." He grabbed his keys from the table.

"Where are you going?"

"To Jake's."

"Why?"

Zach didn't answer at first. He pulled the door open, then looked back at her. "You used me." The door closed with a soft click behind him.

Sharlie collapsed on the couch. She'd sunk as far as she could go.

## Chapter Thirteen

"I didn't sleep with Sharlie."

At the sound of Zach's voice, Logan looked up from the financial report in front of him. He hadn't really been studying it. He'd been staring at the numbers without seeing them. The image of Sharlie coming out of Zach's bedroom remained imbedded in his mind. He couldn't focus on anything else.

He looked at the other man, reading the truth in his eyes. He nodded, indicating the chair in front of his desk. "Have a seat."

Zach sat down, a wary look in his eyes. "Look, I don't know what's going on with you and Sharlie, but I want you to know there's nothing going on between us."

Logan shook his head. "I don't know what's going on between Sharlie and me either."

"I thought you two were going to make it work."

"Yeah." Logan's laugh held no humor. "So did I. We finally talked. About a lot of things we should have talked about a long time ago."

"She told me you asked her to marry you."

"She said no." Saying the words sharpened the pain he'd been carrying around since he'd asked her. Her refusal cut like a knife. He'd never imagined she'd say no.

Maybe she hadn't forgiven him for thinking she'd had an abortion. But he didn't think so. Not when they'd finally gotten everything out in the open. He thought they'd put the past behind them and were ready to move on.

A big part of the puzzle was why she wanted

him to think she'd slept with Zach. It didn't make any sense.

"Yeah, she told me."

Zach's voice brought him back to the present.

"Why would she want me to think she'd slept with you?" Voicing the question didn't bring Logan any closer to an answer.

"I don't know. She's afraid of something."

"What would she be afraid of?" Even as he asked, Logan knew Zach didn't have the answer to that one either.

"She won't talk to me about it."

Logan laughed again, the bitter sound harsh in the small room. "Well, she sure the hell won't talk to me."

"She loves you."

Instead of being reassured, the words stabbed into Logan. "I'm not sure she does. I thought she did, but now, I just don't know."

Zach looked at him. "I'm sure. I've known her for a while now and, in all that time, she's never gotten involved with anyone. Not until you came back."

"No one?" Logan had a hard time believing that. It had been twelve years.

Zach shrugged. "She's gone out on dates, but she never let anyone get close." He looked away. "Not even me."

"I know how you feel about her," Logan said quietly.

Zach shook his head. "It's not that. Don't get me wrong, I would have jumped at the chance if she'd have given me any indication she was interested."

The other man's honesty struck a chord with Logan. "Maybe she's come to realize she has feelings for you." The thought hurt, but maybe that's what she'd been trying to let him know.

Zach shook his head again. "No. I'm telling you, I know her." He tossed Logan a look. "Maybe not as well as you, but I've never seen her the way she is with you. I can tell just by looking at her. She's been different since you've been around."

"Angry, you mean."

Zach laughed. "Well, at first. I mean now. I've never seen her like this. Like you said, twelve years is a long time. She's had plenty of time, and opportunity, to find someone. She never did. She wasn't interested in anyone until you came back. Maybe she's been waiting for you all these years."

Logan considered the words for a moment. He wanted to believe what Zach said, but something still wasn't right. Sharlie hadn't been glad to see him when he'd come back. True, the whole issue with the check from her father had gotten in the way at first. Then she'd been scared to tell him about giving their baby up for adoption. They'd made it through those things.

Something else had made her say no. Something deeper.

Logan stood. "I have to try to talk to her again."

Zach rose as well. "She's still at my place. There's a key on top of the light in the hallway." He paused. "In case she won't let you in the door."

Logan grimaced.

"Don't give up on her."

"I won't." Logan turned in the doorway. "And Zach? Thank you."

The other man smiled. "You're welcome."

****

Sharlie heard a key in the door and, glad Zach had returned, rushed into the living room. She needed to make things right with him before she left. "Zach?"

"It's not Zach."

"Logan." She stopped, her heart hammering against her ribs. He'd come back. "What are you doing here?"

"Isn't that obvious?" He took a step toward her.

She backed away and shook her head.

"I want to talk to you. I think you owe me that." Once more he advanced.

"Please, Logan."

"Please, Logan, what?"

Sharlie backed away as he stalked her. The anger she'd expected wasn't there. He looked determined. Which was worse.

"I...I can't."

"You can't what? Talk about why you said no when I asked you to marry me? Or you can't tell me why you keep things from me, why you lie to me?"

Backed against Zach's coffee table, she didn't have anywhere else to go. "Don't," she said when he reached out. Her voice trembled. She'd come undone if he touched her.

"Sharlie, I love you. You can't run far enough away to hide from that." Despite her protest he grasped her shoulders in his hands. "I thought we'd put the past behind us. I want to marry you and have a family with you."

Sharlie's control shattered. "Don't you understand? I can't have a family with you."

"No, I don't understand. Why don't you want to be with me?"

"I want to be with you more than anything else in the world."

"Then why won't you—"

"Because I can't have any more children." The words hung in the sudden stillness.

Logan's hands dropped from her shoulders. His shocked gaze met hers. "What?"

It took every bit of strength she had not to look away. Saying the words was more painful than keeping them inside all those years had ever been. She took a deep breath. "I can't have children, Logan." The pain cut deeper into her heart. But at least it was out in the open now.

He still looked shell-shocked. "But you—"

"There were complications."

"Complications?"

Sharlie couldn't bear the look in his eyes any longer. She turned away, wrapping her arms around herself. "After I gave birth to our baby and gave her up for adoption," her voice broke, but she forced herself to go on, "I didn't heal right. I developed an infection." She hated how clinical it sounded. "There wasn't anything they could do. I had to have a hysterectomy."

Silence greeted her words.

And stretched on.

She wished Logan would say something, anything. The stillness was stifling. She couldn't even hear him breathing.

Not able to stand it anymore, she risked a glance over her shoulder.

Anguish swam in the depths of his eyes. Tears coursed freely down his cheeks, but he made no effort to hide them. His gaze captured and held hers.

Tears streamed from Sharlie's eyes as well, as she turned to face him. Her gaze took in every inch of his face, committing it to memory, for surely now, he'd turn and walk out of her life forever.

He took a deep breath and tilted his head back, looking up at the ceiling for endless moments. When he finally spoke, his words were unexpected. "Why did you want me to think you slept with Zach?"

Sharlie was caught off guard. "What?"

Logan's gaze came back to hers, but he remained silent.

Sharlie hugged herself. "I thought it would be easier."

"Easier?"

She nodded. "I knew we couldn't be together, because of...because of what's wrong with me, but I didn't know how to tell you. I figured if you were mad at me, it wouldn't matter. I wouldn't have to figure out how to tell you. You wouldn't want me anymore." The words sounded inane, but she didn't know what else to say.

He cursed and turned away from her. "That's the most asinine thing I've ever heard." He pivoted around again, running his fingers through his hair. "So what do we do now?"

"What?"

"What happens now?"

Sharlie was at a loss. Logan wasn't reacting the way she'd expected. "Nothing."

"Nothing?"

"You'll walk out of here. That will be it."

Logan smiled, but it was sad. "You've got it all figured out."

"Isn't that what you want to do?"

"How do you know what I want to do?"

"I thought..."

"Oh, Sharlie, aren't we past all this? Can't we trust each other?"

He stepped closer, his eyes looking deeply into hers. "Is that what you think of me? That I would leave you because of this?"

She shook her head. "I don't know." Unable to force her gaze away from the pain in his, she whispered, "How can you stand to look at me?"

"Looking at you makes me ache."

The agony in her soul threatened to tear her apart. "Because you hate me."

He took both of her hands in his. "Because when you hurt, I hurt. Because you've carried this burden by yourself all these years. Because you felt you couldn't share it with me. Because you thought it would change the way I feel about you." He paused. "If you're going to be my wife, you'll have to learn to trust me."

It took a moment for his words to sink in. "You still want to marry me?" Sharlie couldn't hide the note of incredulity in her voice.

"More than anything else in the world." He smiled softly.

The words, coupled with the look on Logan's face took her breath away. But she couldn't accept them. "I can't give you a family. That's what you want more than anything else in the world."

Logan shook his head, stepping closer to her to cup the side of her face in his hand.

She trembled. His touch felt so good, a salve on her bruised spirit.

"That's not true, and even if it were, it wouldn't matter. Sharlie, if you're not in my life, I don't want to live it."

"Don't say that."

Logan continued as if he hadn't heard her. "We can still have a family."

"But—"

"We can adopt a baby."

"Adopt a baby?" It sounded so absurd considering her past.

"Yes, but only if that's what you want to do. If it's not something you think you can do, then we won't."

"But you always wanted a big family."

"All I ever wanted, from the moment I laid eyes on you, was you. I was seventeen, but I knew it. I knew we belonged together, you and me. And after all these years, after all the hell we've been through, we're finally together, and that's enough for me. Don't throw it away."

As wonderful as the words sounded, she couldn't let him settle for something less than what he'd always wanted. "If we adopted a baby, it wouldn't be ours. We'd have someone else's baby."

"No." His soft whisper caressed her soul. "It

would be ours. Just like our baby is in a loving home, we could give a child a loving home. Genetics can't make you love someone. Look at your father. Look at my mother. Not exactly paragons of parenthood. We share blood with them, but they never knew the meaning of real love. Love comes from in here." He placed his hand over her heart. "From inside, from who we are.

"You showed me what love was all those years ago. I didn't believe in love until I met you. You're so full of love, Sharlie. You'd make a great mother." He paused. "I'm not asking you to be a mother. We can deal with that later. I'm asking you to be my wife."

Logan's words purged the demons from her soul. Tears rolled unchecked down her cheeks. He wiped them away with the gentle stoke of his thumb.

"And I'm asking you to trust me. When something's bothering you, when you're hurting, talk to me. Can you do that?"

Sharlie nodded, then inhaled a deep, shuddering breath. "I love you, Logan."

He drew her into his embrace. Sharlie clung to him, savoring the feel of his arms around her. She felt safe and secure and protected. Whatever came at them in the future, they would face together.

He pulled back, his eyes probing hers once again. "I love you, Sharlie. Will you marry me?"

The love she saw shining in his eyes chased the last of her fears away. She laid a hand against his face. This time the touch didn't need to last for a lifetime. She knew he'd be hers for that long.

"Yes," she whispered.

He closed his eyes for a moment. When opened them, Sharlie saw the promise of eternity reflected in their depths. He reached into his pocket and retrieved the ring he'd offered her two nights ago. "Once I put this on your finger, it's never coming off. Are you sure?"

"Oh, yes."

Logan slipped the ring on her finger, then brought her hand to his mouth for a searing kiss. He grinned. "It's a good thing you said yes. I wasn't going to ask a third time," he teased.

Sharlie laughed for the sheer, unadulterated pleasure of it and threw her arms around his neck. She kissed him fiercely, feeling desire flare in her stomach when he deepened the kiss, pulling her so close to the heat of his body she swore their hearts beat as one.

**\*\*\*\***

"You look beautiful, honey."

Sharlie smiled up at the man at her side. "Thanks, Pete." She adjusted the gauzy veil lying over her hair and smoothed her hands down the folds of the full, white satin gown one last time. Even though she and Logan had planned a small wedding, she couldn't resist wearing a traditional dress. She had waited to become his wife for so long, she wanted everything to be perfect.

Someone handed her a fragrant bouquet. With her other hand she grasped Pete's arm.

"You ready?" he questioned as the first strains of *The Wedding March* filled the air.

Sharlie nodded.

"Then let's do it." He winked at her.

"Thanks for giving me away."

Pete kissed her on the cheek. "I wouldn't have missed it for the world."

They glided down the petal-strewn path toward Logan, who waited beneath a high arch of flowers.

Sharlie caught her breath at how handsome he looked in his formal black tuxedo. He stood sure and bold against the backdrop of mountains in the distance. Strong enough to handle anything that ever came their way.

Pete released her to her groom as they came to

the end of the aisle. The reassuring feel of Logan's hand as he held hers confirmed that she would never face anything alone again. His eyes swept over her, telling her without words how beautiful he thought she was.

"Dearly beloved," began the minister facing them.

The words of the ceremony drifted over her as if from a dream. She couldn't quite believe it was happening.

The way Logan's husky "I do" found its way deep into her heart and soul told her it was real.

Her whispered promise soon followed his. He slipped a slender gold ring onto her finger. It nestled next to the diamond he had placed there. She pushed his wide band into place, her eyes never straying from the love mirrored in his.

"I now pronounce you husband and wife. You may kiss the bride."

Logan framed Sharlie's face in his hands, the pad of his thumb brushing away the lone tear trickling down her cheek.

"I love you," he whispered into the heat of her mouth, before his lips took possession of hers. The kiss sealed anew every promise that had been spoken between them.

"I love you, Logan," she said when he pulled away.

"I now present to you, Mr. and Mrs. Logan Reed."

The small assembly of guests gathered in the backyard broke into applause.

Pete was the first to grab Sharlie in a huge bear hug. "Congratulations, sweetheart."

"Thanks." She laughed with unrestrained joy.

Her smile faded as she saw Zach rise from his chair and head around the side of the house without approaching her. She hadn't forgiven herself for hurting him, and she needed to make things right.

Less than two weeks had passed since Logan had proposed. They'd both decided they didn't want to wait any longer than necessary to get married. Twelve years was long enough.

Sharlie had been busy with arrangements and hadn't spent much time at The Corral. Which meant she hadn't seen much of Zach.

They hadn't had a chance to sit down and talk, which troubled her. She didn't want to lose his friendship. The thought was the only dark spot on an otherwise glorious day.

Chapter Fourteen

Later, Logan held her against him as they danced. The parquet floor of The Corral was empty, save for the newly wedded couple.

"Have I told you how beautiful you look today, Mrs. Reed?"

Sharlie nodded, relishing the compliment almost as much as the sound of her new name. "I like the sound of that," she said, smiling up at her husband.

"So do I, honey. So do I." He kissed her, his eyes holding the promise of passion to come.

The ballad ended and applause filled the air. The dance floor filled with other couples. Sharlie glimpsed Zach across the room.

She smiled up at Logan. "Would you please get me something to drink? I need to talk to someone."

"Sure, sweetheart." He dropped another kiss on her lips and strolled away.

Sharlie straightened her shoulders and went in search of Zach. She found him standing by the side bar.

"Hi."

He turned, a wary smile of greeting on his face.

"Come sit and talk with me." Sharlie linked her arm through his, guiding him toward a far table. "I haven't seen you much these past few days."

"I'm sure you've had other things on your mind." Zach held out a chair for her.

"Don't do this, Zach.

"Do what?"

"Don't pull away from me." She reached across the table to take his hand in hers. "I'm sorry I hurt

164

you. I wasn't thinking straight. You've been part of my life for a long time. I don't want that to change. Can we still be friends?"

Zach's gaze skipped across the room, then returned to hers. "Are you sure your husband is okay with that?"

She didn't answer right away, but looked at her friend. He had been avoiding her, and it wasn't all because of what she'd done. She knew he was trying to figure out where he fit into the new life she was making with Logan. She had to find some way to reassure him.

"I wanted to thank you."

Zach looked taken aback. "For what?"

"For helping Logan and me. If you hadn't talked to him, we might not be here today. You're a good friend. We're both lucky to have you for a friend."

"I couldn't stand the thought of you hurting. I knew Logan was the one who could make you happy. He loves you."

This time she was the surprised one.

Zach chuckled. "I'm not blind, you know. Any fool can tell how the man feels by the way he looks at you." He sighed. "I want you to be happy."

"I am happy. I love Logan. I've never loved anyone else."

Zach nodded.

"But you're still my friend. I couldn't imagine my life if you weren't in it, too."

"I'll be here as long as you want me to be."

"You forgive me then?"

He squeezed her hand. "Yes."

"Thank you. You know, someday you're going to find someone who realizes what a wonderful man you are. And when that happens, she's never going to let you go."

"I hope you're right."

"I always am."

Zach laughed. "And modest, too. What would I do without you?"

"Well, like I said, you won't have to find out."

He gave her hand one more affectionate squeeze, then rose from his chair. "May I dance with the bride?"

She smiled and nodded. "I'd love to."

****

Logan saw Zach pull Sharlie into his arms on the dance floor. She looked like a beautiful, fairy tale princess. And he was going to do his damnedest to make sure all her dreams came true.

The song ended, and he walked out onto the floor.

Desire knotted his stomach as Sharlie smiled up at him. All she had to do was look at him and he was aroused. At the same time his heart ached as he thought about all she had gone through since they'd been apart. He'd move hell itself to ensure she wasn't hurt again.

"Hi."

"Hi, yourself."

"Congratulations, Logan." Zach held out his hand. "You're a lucky man."

Logan shook the proffered hand. "Thanks." He drew Sharlie close to his side. "I'll take good care of her."

Zach chuckled. "I know you will."

The night passed with amazing quickness. Before Logan knew it, the DJ announced the bride needed to take her place for the traditional bouquet toss.

Logan watched as all of the single women in the room flooded onto the dance floor behind Sharlie.

"She's the prettiest one out there," Pete said, coming to stand beside Logan.

"I agree, but then I'm biased," he said with a smile, never taking his eyes from his bride.

"I think we all are."

On the floor, Sharlie moved to the sexy rhythm of the music, her gown billowing around her. Logan's thoughts drifted to later on that night when he'd be able to slide the dress from her body and make love to her.

His body reacted immediately to the thought. Heat coursed through him, and he shifted his legs uncomfortably, glad for the dim lighting in the room.

One of the waitresses from The Corral caught the bouquet and squealed in delight. Logan barely noticed. He had eyes only for Sharlie.

"Now you get to have some fun," Jake said, coming to stand beside him, a lecherous grin on his face. "Time to remove the garter."

Logan almost groaned. How was he going to manage that without going insane? His gaze caught and held Sharlie's as he made his way onto the floor amid loud whoops and catcalls. Her eyes sparkled with delight, as if anticipating his touch on her skin.

He knelt on the floor in front of her, his glance skimming over her face, then down over the pristine white wedding gown to the tips of her shoes, which peeked out from beneath the hem.

He raised the dress, then ducked his head beneath the wide bell of the skirt. With one hand he held the satin away from him. With the other he grasped her slim ankle. He traced a line up her shapely calf with the tip of his tongue. She tensed.

Good. Now she knew how he felt.

He nipped the back of her knee, then drew his open mouth up past the garter and across the lace top of her stocking until he reached bare skin. He sucked the soft flesh on the inside of her thigh before moving back down to the beribboned garter. With his teeth, he drew it down her leg, relishing the feel of her trembling against his mouth.

The fancy bit of elastic and lace caught between

his teeth, he emerged from beneath her skirt and grinned up into Sharlie's flushed face.

The beating of his heart nearly drowned out the sound of the wolf whistles all around as he dropped the garter and brought her lips down to meet his. He kept the kiss brief. His body couldn't take much more holding back. He wanted her. Now.

Taking a deep breath and hoping his tuxedo jacket and the dim lighting would once again disguise the evidence of his desire, Logan rose to his feet. The single men present had gathered to one side of the floor. He turned his back and circled the garter over his head several times, then let it go with a flick of his wrist.

The beribboned missile sailed through the air across the expanse of parquet and landed in Zach's hands. His head jerked up. Then he grinned. "Well, what do you know?"

Next to Logan, Sharlie laughed in delight. "See?" she said to Zach. "I told you so."

The last dance of the night was announced.

Logan swept Sharlie into his arms, pulling her close, letting her feel the hard imprint of his body.

Her eyes widened, then softened with teasing lights. "That's what you get for doing that to me."

"Doing what?" he asked innocently. He teased the side of her neck with feather-light touches of his lips, oblivious to those dancing nearby.

Sharlie gasped and sagged against him. He drew her closer.

"I want to take you home right now," he ground out between clenched teeth, as her mouth mimicked his actions against the flesh above his collar. "Come on." He grabbed her hand and pulled her from the dance floor.

"Logan, we can't," Sharlie protested as he led her through the throng of people.

"We're newlyweds. I'm sure they'll understand,"

Logan said with determination. "I'm taking you home. I want to make love to my wife."

****

Flickering candlelight danced over the planes of Logan's face as he stood before Sharlie in their bedroom. His tuxedo jacket, along with his tie and cummerbund, lay discarded across a nearby chair. Her filmy veil lay atop it all.

Her breath caught as he undid the tiny buttons on his shirt. Even in the dim light, his tanned skin contrasted sharply with the crisp white cotton. His impatience evident, he tossed the cufflinks aside, then shrugged out of the shirt, letting it fall to the floor.

The sight of his muscled chest started her pulse pounding. He stepped toward her, closing the distance between them. She trembled as he gently turned her away from him. He unfastened the long row of buttons running the length of her back, kissing each inch of flesh he bared. She shuddered at the moist heat of his mouth against her spine.

The dress fell to the floor with a soft rustle, leaving her clad in tiny lace panties, thigh-high silk stockings, and white satin pumps. She heard him suck in a deep breath, feeling the warm rush of air against her bare skin as he exhaled. She stepped out of the dress and turned to face him.

His glittering gaze slid down her bare body. The heat from his look warmed her flesh, but at the same time raised goosebumps along her arms. He captured her face in his hands, bringing her lips to his in a devastating kiss. He deepened the contact, his tongue sliding into her mouth to duel with hers in a sensual dance. At the same time he brought their bodies closer so they touched from chest to thigh.

Sharlie's nipples tightened when they brushed his crisp, curling chest hair. She moaned. An answering groan rumbled deep inside Logan as she pressed even closer, letting him feel the hardened tips of her breasts against him.

He scooped her into his arms and laid her across the wide bed. He followed her down, stretching his body next to hers. Propping himself on one elbow, he traced a fiery path down her body. He skimmed the valley between her breasts down to the waistband of her panties. He slid his hand beneath the elastic and dragged the skimpy garment down her legs. His hand trembled as it followed a path back up one silk-covered leg, over the concave dip of her abdomen, to cup one quivering breast.

Sharlie arched into his palm. The nipple tightened further as his mouth dipped to suckle her. Her breath came in small pants when his teeth grazed over the sensitive flesh before turning his attention to its twin. Her hands roamed over the exposed skin of his back until his waistband stopped further exploration.

With shaking fingers she fumbled with the clasp of his pants until it opened. She eased the zipper down over straining flesh. She took him in her hands as soon as he was free.

He groaned and, with clumsy movements, divested himself of the rest of his clothing. "God, Sharlie. You don't know what you do to me."

She managed a grin, although her insides were on fire. "I think I have a good idea." She gasped as Logan's hands and lips returned to her breast. The erotic tug of his mouth ravaged her senses until she was mindless.

"Please," she begged. "I can't wait anymore."

He rolled her beneath him and parted her legs with gentle pressure from his own. He slid slowly into her, then nearly out again. She cried out in pleasure as the pulsating rhythm continued. She gripped him with her arms and legs to draw him deeper. It had never felt this good before. Knowing she was his wife made everything stronger, hotter.

His harsh breathing sent fevered caresses down her body. The tension increased, until a shiver wracked her entire body. She let go, spiraling out of control. The heavens exploded behind her eyes. Logan shuddered over her in release.

"I love you," he managed in a hoarse whisper.

"I love you, too." She kissed his damp brow when her raging emotions had calmed. Then she cuddled against him in the tangled bedding.

****

Hours later, Logan stirred when she moved away from him.

"Where are you going?" The sleepy, satisfied tone of his voice washed over her.

"I have something for you." Sharlie slipped out of bed to retrieve a small, wrapped box from the top dresser drawer. She handed it to him, then slid back under the covers, pulling them up around her as she sat on the bed facing him.

Logan propped himself up against the headboard. "I thought we decided not to get each other anything."

"It's not really a wedding present."

He untied the ribbon from the box and tore off the paper, then lifted the lid. His breath hitched as he stared at the contents. "Oh, Sharlie."

His shaking fingers reached in to pull out the tiny hospital bracelet. He removed the framed photograph from inside the box as well. He looked at the graduation picture for long moments before his gaze sought hers. Tears glimmered in his eyes but didn't fall.

She swallowed. "In that picture I was..."

"She was inside you?"

Sharlie nodded, unable to speak.

Logan's attention returned to the items in his

171

hand. "Thank you." His voice trembled. A tear ran down his cheek.

She caressed his face with her palm, brushing the tear away with her fingertip. "I didn't mean to make you sad."

Logan looked deep into her eyes. "I couldn't be any happier than I am at this moment."

The words curled into Sharlie's heart and soul. The past was finally behind them and, whatever the future threw at them, they'd face together.

Secure in the promise of his love, she snuggled down into the bed next to him. This time for always.

# About the Author

Debra St. John has been reading and writing romance since high school. She always dreamed about publishing a romance novel some day. *This Time for Always* is her first published work of fiction. She lives in a suburb of Chicago with her husband, who is her real life hero. Debra is past president of her local RWA chapter and has also served in the capacity of advisor, manuscript chair, and secretary.

You're invited to visit Debra at her website, www.debrastjohnromance.com,
or at the Acme Author's Link,
http://acmeauthorslink.blogspot.com, where she is the Sunday Blogger.